BUTTERFLY STOMP WALTZ

Michael Warren Lucas

Thanks to Rebecca Bates, Peter Jeremy, Bonnie Koenig, Matthew Kroll, Kate MacLeod, Mark Moellering, Lucy A Snyder, and Brian Powell for invaluable opinions on earlier versions of this book.

A special thanks to Cylithria Dubois, for her comparative analysis of broken ribs.

This book exists because Kris Rusch told me to write it. Don't argue with Kris. You won't get anywhere. It's best just to shut up and do what the nice lady tells you.

As always, this is for Liz.

The plan: break into Butterfly Star Research. Steal the data, research and processes for their incomplete, suppressed sickle-cell cure. Make everything as public and explicit as a fading starlet's professionally-shot sex tape. Miller Time.

I'd rather get a Blue Moon, but "blue moon time" means something totally different. You get a doctorate in astrophysics before your twenty-third birthday, they teach you these things.

I still had to learn about betrayal and lies on my own, though.

Say "Billie Carrie Salton" in the right places, usually rancid bars on the wrong side of town or even more rancid corporate boardrooms, and people dive under the table and bawl for momma. Say it in the wrong places, and they'll either say "Can we afford her?" or "How do you know Beaks?" (BCS, get it?) The FBI has my picture on their wall, right next to my description. Six foot one (too tall), one-sixty pounds. Sharp nose that has nothing to do with my nickname. Size eleven feet. Blonde, redhead, brunette, or sometimes spumoni. There's one agent with a real hard-on for my head, and another with a bigger hard-on for all the rest of me.

Fun times.

So fine, I'm a killer. Get in my way, this Detroit-born girl will put you down hard.

But I've never murdered a hostage or bystander who didn't make a move first. You get cute, I'll give you a third eye before the eyes you came with can blink. Behave yourself, stay quiet in that back room till the cops find their map and their flashlight, you'll get home safe. Probably get on TV and a few days off work and the sympathy vote. I even let this one kid's poodle live, and I *really* wanted to punt that little monster out the great big hole we burned in that thirty-third floor window.

I've never robbed anyone of anything that wasn't stolen.

Too bad the whole country's been stolen.

Along with the rest of the world.

Which takes me back to Butterfly Star.

Sickle cell anemia's really horrible. You *hurt*. Sometimes you fall over in agony, no warning, just *pow* and you're down. Your body can't fight off infections so well. You'll probably die in agony before you're fifty. It killed a high school friend of mine before he even got his driver's license. Add in the fact that it's hereditary and found mostly in blacks and folks from the Middle East. You've got these people at the bottom, who're supposed to work hard and pull themselves up by their bootstraps, except for the little detail that every so often they keel over screaming in pain and get fired.

Butterfly took federal funds to research sickle cell.

A lot of federal funds.

My sources tell me that their researchers learned some interesting things, and even made progress on a cure. It's not perfect—nothing ever is—but in the sickle cell puzzle it's a couple corners and enough connected middle pieces that you can make out the horse's ass.

When you get a degree in a science, like astrophysics or genetic diseases, they tell you the scientific method has four steps. Observation. Hypothesis. Test. Conclusions.

But culturally, science has a fifth step.

Publish.

It's not science if you don't tell people what you learn. If you don't let others build on your work. Otherwise, you're just playing solitaire with Petri dishes.

Butterfly didn't solve the whole thing, so they didn't manufacture a cure.

But the data—ah, the data's valuable. Not now, sure, but one day, when someone else puts most of the puzzle together, they'll whip out the corner pieces and their horse's ass and shout "We cured sickle cell! We win!" Never mind that some bright young thing in a podunk med school right now, *tonight*, might look at the Butterfly data and jump the whole thing forward ten years.

Save thousands of lives, and years of agony.

If they'd done this on their own dime, fine. Don't get me wrong, they'd still be jackasses, but I couldn't really say they didn't have the right to do it. You buy the cards, play all the solitaire you want. They'd done their research with federal funds, though. Our taxes paid for that knowledge.

All right, fine. *Your* taxes.

Still.

That knowledge belongs to everyone.

Normally I'd call some people I know and put a raid together. There's no profit in this, though—it's a straight smash-and-grab-and-upload. I've got a few special people who owe me big, but calling in those favors on a gig like this would be slicing watermelon with a cement truck. And after last week's Newcastle debacle, my budget was the change in the back seat of my rusty grungy black Econoliner van and the gear I'd accumulated in the last four years.

Fortunately, it's some pretty awesome gear.

So that's why I'm hugging the outside of the forty-first floor of the glass-walled Embassy Building, letting the wind whistle through my hollow head.

It's easy to trust equipment when I'm five or ten feet off the ground. Ten, twenty, thirty floors, no problem. Forty-one floors, though, and my trust gets a little shaky. I wear skin-tight jumpsuits on climbing gigs because the wind can't whistle up inside them, not because they showcase my great big butt. (Okay, people tell me it's tiny, but when you're in a skin-tight jumpsuit, your butt is huge.) At that height the wind, without any trees or all those pesky buildings to slow it down, feels pretty vicious and carries all these nasty smells of exhaust and smoke and diesel and burned jet fuel. The smells come and go, so when I get used to one reek another flavor digs in. Up here, even the air feels like it wants to slap me down like a leaf, especially when there's nothing whatsoever under that aforementioned butt and I'm carrying a forty-pound pack.

I'm wearing traction pads on my knees and elbows, bootlegged from a nonexistent Special Forces unit returning from an Unnamed Friendly Country. The pads hold the glass like they've been nailed there, until I work the toggle strapped to my left palm. Detach one pad, raise one limb, lock it back down. Right leg, left hand, left leg, right hand. Lift with your legs, never your arms.

Repeat.

I'd stretched for an hour before starting this climb, and my hips and shoulders and elbows still grind and pull like frayed belts on dying machines.

In Georgia's July heat, this glass almost sweats. This high-tech stuff was supposed to clean itself every time it rains, but pollution and condensation still make it greasy and gritty. It isn't supposed to bother the traction pads. I'd never seen the faintest hint of anything bothering the traction pads.

Maybe slick glass doesn't bother the traction pads, but it sure bothers me.

The Embassy Building's way outside Atlanta, in this chunk of green space and private homes and convenience stores and dentist offices. Atlanta looks like a tangle of Christmas lights, mostly white but with reds and blues and greens all mixed up in there. Christmas is the wrong holiday, though. The fireworks for the Fourth ended a couple hours ago, except for the occasional low sparkle across the countryside where some drunk good old boy has decided it's okay to piss off the neighbors after midnight. The eight-lane highways run out, individual headlights invisible from up there but all together giving this subliminal impression of slow-flowing light.

For just a moment, looking out at those inverted constellations, I feel even farther above everyone.

Don't get me wrong, I'm not *worth* more than anyone else. I'm smarter, yeah. Faster. Stronger. The right side of the bell curve is this itty-bitty little dot receding in my rear view mirror. But that's all genetics.

I'm not *worth* more than anyone.

Except the scumbags pillaging the planet, of course.

The sky is clear, moonless, but the city's light pollution eats all the stars except Sirius.

What with slithering around the lit windows I'd crawled the equivalent of maybe forty-eight, forty-nine floors to get to the forty-first. But I needed this window right here. I uncouple my right hand from the traction pad, cautiously shake my arm to loosen that elbow and wrist and knuckles without losing my three points on, and pull out the cutting tool. Each generation of glass gets harder to cut, yes, but the cutting tools get better too. There's tools to lift a whole big window pane out of its frame, gentle as brushing a baby's hair, and put it back in so smooth nobody knows how you got in. But they're slow and annoying.

Truth to tell, I don't give a damn if they figure out how I'd got in. I only care that the alarms on this floor aren't active.

Attach the palm-sized disk of the cutter to the glass, right in the center of the hole I want.

Extend the cutting arm and the two anchor arms.

Touch cutter to glass.

Push the button.

The anchors glomp onto the glass. The cutter rotates on its own, making one pass to score the glass, then digging deep. I feel this faint vibration through the pads, not enough to shake my teeth but enough to set up a resonance in my spine. My chiropractor's gonna love this.

Glass turns back to sand and skitters out of the cut, the wind whipping sand and smell away before they can add to the irritation in my sinuses. Yes, I have allergies—thank God for steroid nose spray, or people would call me Snots instead of Beaks.

The sight of the turning cutter suddenly tightens my heart, and under my goggles I have to blink away tears.

Dammit, not now, I told myself. *Not the time.*

I'd taken the cutter from Deke's gear. After Newcastle.

You got hammered. You mourned him. Moving on.

He would have wanted me to.

Risks of the job. He knew it.

I grit my teeth. There's better things to think of. Like sickle cell anemia cures, and the bastards who don't want you to have them.

I moved a couple feet to the left while the cutter turned. The glass wasn't going to fall towards me—even if I wasn't ethical, having a three-foot disk of glass plunge five hundred feet out of the sky onto the sidewalk or some bastard's Tesla or just half-bury itself edge-on in a little stretch of starving grass imprisoned in concrete would attract attention up here. It's not going to fall, but I didn't get here by taking stupid chances (Deke) that might get me killed.

I force myself to breathe deeply and concentrate on a spot between and just above my eyebrows. Any amateur can meditate on a cushion, but it takes *real* discipline to hold the thought with forty-one stories of open air between your butt and the cushion.

It's a long five minutes before the window ripples with this "pop" that I feel through the pads more than I hear, and a gust of cool dry air hisses past me from the paper-thin cut. The cutter arm rotates once more and the whole window vibrates as a three-foot wide disk of glass snaps free.

The sturdy glass stands in place, balanced on its two-inch edge. The cutter's super-suction braces won't let it fall out, but it can't topple in until the air pressure equalizes a little more. It's maybe thirty seconds until the hissing stops and I can reach out and tap the last button on the cutter's central unit.

The disk of glass leans inward in exaggerated slow motion, then hits the tipping point and thuds into the dark interior.

With the ingress right there, my strained shoulders and hip are screaming for me to slip through the hole and use some other muscle, any other muscle. I free my right arm again to meticulously retract the cutter's cutting arm, then hit a button to detach the anchor on the far side of the hole. I retract the whole cutter to the anchor right next to me, where I can easily pull all its arms in and snap it to my belt before detaching the last anchor.

I am not losing this cutter. Not ever. Even if better comes out.

Only once I have everything snugged back onto my belt do I slide over to the window. I turn the infra-red vision in my goggles up to ten percent and peer in.

Nobody's there.

I flip the goggles back to normal vision.

The hole is exactly wide enough for my pack and I to slither into the building's darkness.

3

I don't believe in cranking up the night vision everywhere you go. Sure, you get this nice green hazy view of damn near everything. It's great for some situations. But in a raid like this, someone turns on the lights and you're blind for half a second.

And while your eyes adjust, some rent-a-cop shoots you.

You're better off with the human eye. We're descended from a long line of people who didn't get eaten by lions and tigers and bears, at least not before they had kids. I haven't had kids, so I'm safe.

It's a joke, people. Chill. Sheesh.

The glass disk lays at an angle, so I slip down it and plant my high-traction waffle-tread parachute-cord-laced leather boots on the smooth barren concrete next to it. As my eyes adjust, the dark bowels of the Embassy Building's forty-first floor coalesce from the darkness. The building management company's system said that some wealth management assholes rented this floor a few months ago and totally gutted it so they could put in fancier and more expensive walls. Looking around I see flashes of the glass exterior all around me, sliced by all these irregular vertical lines. The contractors had gotten the aluminum studs up for the interior walls, but the glass and wallboard wasn't yet hung.

The place stinks of industrial glue and solvents, passing my face in a steady stream through the hole in the glass at my back. It's the smell of good honest labor, real people doing real work with real skill, for not enough money, and going home to try to give the families they love a better life.

Once those smells wore off, the place would stink of perfume and corruption.

Standing sparks flames from my toes all the way up my spine. My feet had dangled from my knees for the last hour and a half, and now I suddenly made them do all the work. My knees and hips demand their union-contracted break, and my elbows threaten a sympathy strike if I don't ditch the clunky traction pads. The shoulders demand I ditch the pack while I'm at it.

I hold myself still, though, and study the room.

The red and white beacon of an EXI sign, the last letter cloaked by a tangle of cables drooping from the ceiling. Tiny green LEDs gleam from the central stack, where the elevator and the wiring and the water transfix the floor and ceiling. Scattered dots of red LEDs from the smoke detectors and the carbon monoxide detectors, still active even during construction. Aluminum ventilation shafts, too narrow to crawl through and too thin to stop bullets, hug the ceiling and reflect sharp lines of light.

A few feet before me, sawhorses shape the shadows. A square thing a little smaller than a kitchen cabinet lurks to my left. One edge of the severed glass plug had landed on it, tipping the glass at a good fifty-two degrees or so. A tool chest?

But the space to my right is open and clean.

I sink to my knees on the warm concrete with a sigh of simple pleasure and shrug out of the backpack's shoulders and hip belt. I unbuckle the traction pad from my right elbow, and the skin beneath it suddenly seems to steam beneath the skintight suit. The pad goes into a special pouch on the outside of the backpack, and the other three pads follow. From the bottom part of the backpack, I stash my climbing belt and pull out the one with my penetration tools: a couple special-purpose microcomputers, lock picks, a silenced tiny .38 semi-auto, a couple other breaking-and-entering gadgets.

I figure that was Batman's secret, too. He didn't put everything on his utility belt. He kept a separate utility belt for each villain. Always learn from the greats.

Then I rotate my legs into the splits and start turning my shoulders to work out the strains.

In the movies, someone climbs a building and charges straight off to disarm the alarm system before getting into a firefight and blowing up the place. People reload their guns and neatly stow their electronic countermeasure devices, but they forget that their greatest weapon, their most powerful tool, is their own body. When you push yourself to your limits, find a secure location and take a moment or two to loosen up.

In a couple minutes the splits get comfortable, so I stretch my feet straight out in front and lower my head between them, pushing my arms further out, straightening my spine. My left hand brushes a stray socket wrench, but I ease my fingers past it. Fingerprints don't worry me—my gloves are this incredible synthetic stuff, high-traction, breathable, and totally resistant to stains. Picked them up at Costco. Advertised for use with cell phone touchscreens. They probably work okay for that, too, but I use a phone with a physical keypad when I'm on the job.

In a few minutes I float to my feet, joints free and muscles relaxed. The tool belt clips around my waist, the backpack on my back, everything carefully secured and tucked inside light-absorbing dark green cloth that matches my jumpsuit. I feel like I've just had a massage.

The central stack of a business tower holds the building's vitals, like the elevator shafts and the great big sewage and water pipes. The Embassy's builders had thought ahead, though, even back when they built this place, and right next to the elevator they'd put in this ten-foot shaft just for wiring.

The wiring shaft has a mechanical lock, and an alarm. You don't want your wiring shaft on the building's swipe card system, because if the swipe card wiring breaks and the door locks you can't get at it to fix it. It's keyed on both sides, so maintenance people can use a key to leave the wiring shaft. So they usually put a pretty decent lock on the door—a high-end Schlage in this case.

It's a tough lock. I need a whole three minutes to pick it. I carry a Lock-Release in my bag, this gun-like thing law enforcement uses to automatically open locks. It works, but having to use it makes me feel like I've failed, and I'm not in a hurry tonight.

The wiring shaft is lit with these old fluorescent tubes, one on every floor. There's kind of a floor. It's a metal grid with wire panels, kind of like a drop ceiling you can see through. The floor panels near the corrugated concrete walls are all removed so these tie-wrapped or twine-bound bundles of dozens of different types of wire can pass up and down. Two holes in opposite sides of the shaft, each the size of a dinner plate, act as pass-throughs for this floor's wiring. A clean new bundle emerges from each hole and pours down through one of the gaps in the floor. Up near the roof, this shaft is pretty empty. Down in the basement, it's a choked claustrophobic nightmare. The wiring shaft stinks of grease and ancient plastic and ages and ages of dust. (All hail the mighty steroid nose spray!)

The wires carry the building's secrets. I could learn so much with a couple carefully placed sniffers.

But the greasy grimy flat metal rungs of the ladder carries me up to the forty-ninth floor and Butterfly Star Research.

4

This is where things get tricky. First, the alarm.

I'm in the wiring shaft, with all the dust and grunge and probably a constant thin rain of asbestos, right outside the access door to Butterfly Star's offices. The alarm cable's pretty clearly marked. It's a gray cable stamped VIGILANTE SECURITY, like they're going to come after me with a six-shooter and a noose. Deke always says—

said—

Never mind.

You can't just cut the wire. Losing the heartbeat signal triggers an alarm back at the security company HQ and activates the local fallback system. Lose both signals, the police get sent out. I have a massively illegal 4G jammer to block the backup, but I would need to get into the office for it to be any use. Disabling this alarm won't stop the fire alarm, that's on a whole separate circuit, but I have no intention of burning this place down.

There's lots of ways to take care of the alarm, lots of toys you can buy from hard-to-find specialists, but I like artificial heartbeats. I slice the plastic sheath over the wire, the long way, exposing the eight color-coded wires within.

The drab gray plastic-cased bypass unit's about the size of an old-fashioned pager with a power button and two little lights. Eight thin wire leads trail from its bottom, each uniquely color-coded, each ending in an alligator clip.

The colors on the bypass unit leads match those on the alarm cable wires.

Even in this dim, dismal lighting, I only need about ten seconds to magnetically stick the bypass to a convenient iron strut, clip each wire to its mate, verify they're secure, and push the button.

The bypass silently analyzes the signal from the alarm box inside Butterfly. In about two minutes, its LED flashes green three times and goes dark.

I snip the alarm wire right above the alligator clips. The bypass unit will silently take over, transmitting the Butterfly heartbeat to the security company.

A really paranoid Butterfly would have a double heartbeat, one going in and one going out. I'm sure management can't imagine anyone stealing their data, especially since nobody knows about it.

Nobody but the researchers, that is.

Researchers like my contact.

No, I won't tell you who. Sheesh!

So: the door.

Butterfly's put a second lock on the access door. The Schlage will take three minutes, maybe less, but the big cylindrical Maximus—

—has already been popped.

From this side.

The access door to the forty-ninth floor isn't *quite* shut all the way.

Someone's already broken into Butterfly Star.

5

Everything changes in a flash.

Standing on this wire mesh floor, with fifty-some airy mesh floors between me and the bottom of the sub-basement, warm oily air rising from below, my heart is suddenly doing triple time.

I hadn't exactly dawdled, but I hadn't done everything as quickly as possible either. I'd climbed the slick glass outside walls at a fairly comfortable pace, taken the time to pick a lock by hand, clambered up the wiring shaft ladder like I was playfully climbing an apple tree. The leisurely stretch had been mandatory, but I could have shaved half an hour or so off of the whole thing.

Butterfly's security people would have checked that access door before they left.

Someone had beat me here.

Illicitly entered through this door.

Tonight.

This gig has gone totally fubar.

Pull out, I think. *Abort.*

Beneath the skintight dark green jumpsuit, a dot of sweat trickles down my spine.

A fine tension ripples down my shoulders, my arms, my legs.

My brain overrides the fight-or-flight impulse.

Every floor of the Embassy Building except forty-one is in use and alarmed. When I'd cut a hole into the glass, the floor still had overpressure. The perps hadn't come in the same way I did. They used the same wiring shaft to enter Butterfly, though. They probably either did a roof entrance with a helicopter, or got working passcards and waltzed right in the front door.

Had the perps killed the security guards? Tied them up? Or were the guards oblivious behind their big desk, eating fries and talking smack?

How had the perps disabled the alarms? Would my circumvention clash with their circumvention? Had I summoned the SWAT team?

And what did the perps want? Was this a smash-and-grab? A quiet exfiltration? Blow out the whole floor?

A squad of testosterone-crazed commandos or one lone sneaky woman?

This is nuts, I think. *Smart thing to do is abort. You're the smart one, remember?*

Whenever a gig slid sideways, whenever the ground rules completely changed halfway through, I'd usually push hard to cancel. Back off, try again. Others (*Deke*) said we should continue, that things always went wrong and that we—*I* had the skills to pull things off.

It's always a decision.

A team decides before they start who gets to make that decision.

I'm the team.

I was going to sleep in the van tonight, no matter what.

The only question was, would I sleep the sleep of the just, or stay awake frustrated that I'd missed my chance?

I'm not usually the angry one.

I guess that's my job now too.

So let's get through that door.

6

Opening an unlocked door is simple. One push and it should swing right open, letting me escape the grungy wiring shaft into Butterfly.

Unless the perps put a Claymore on the other side. No, not a real Claymore. Probably a chunk of plastique, or even a grenade on a string. Some kind of fangy-bangy alarm with teeth. They won't use too much explosive here, though, even if they're on a blowout gig. The wiring shaft is part of the spine of the building, and they won't want to damage it until they're ready to retreat.

They might have a small shaped charge to kill whoever opens the door. Maybe a grenade. Any blast won't go much past the concrete wall.

My utility belt has all kinds of gadgetry, from a cluster of smoke pellets to my .38 semi-auto. I don't like guns, can't stand to use them if there's any other way, but a gun intimidates damn fool civilians faster than anything else. And I practice for a few hours a month, because a weapon you can't use belongs to the other guy. My backpack has another whole set of tools in the bottom compartment, though, and one delightfully special tool in the top.

I climb to the next floor up and pull out my locking extensible pole and a pair of earplugs. It's a little thicker than an old-fashioned TV antenna and a lot stiffer. I extend it one section at a time through the mesh floor until it touches the door.

My heart is pounding.

The door will probably pop open.

Probably.

I let out my breath and push the rod.

The rod bends just a little, scraping against the wire mesh floor.

Tension ripples from the door, through the rod, up into my hand.

Then the far end gives, and the door creaks open an inch.

I ease it a couple more inches, just to be sure, then push it the rest of the way. Some pros mine the backside of the door, so that the blast doesn't go off until you open it wide enough for a person to get through.

I've done that booby-trap myself. It's the right thing to do on some gigs.

But I feel the door bounce against a wall.

I let out my breath. This isn't a kill job. Well, not a blatant one.

I might discover a pressure switch or tripwire beyond the door.

Or these perps are just stupid and sloppy.

Can't tell yet.

So I retract the rod and slip down to find out.

Looking from the filthy grungy wiring shaft through the doorway looks like a glimpse of heaven. Pale industrial-grade carpeting, crapped out by the mile in some Third World hellhole. Bright white walls. The smells of some sharp soap and a hint of pine. Every other lighting panel in the suspended ceiling is half-lit, after-hours illumination almost brilliant after the dismal lighting I have out here.

The gray, tightly woven carpet beyond the door is intact. No pressure plate. I don't see any trigger lasers stuck on the walls, either, or dangling wires that might indicate a poorly planted mine.

So I step into Butterfly and ease the door to behind me, blocking out the shaft's rank greasy dustiness. The bastards who pay for these places don't give a damn if the behind-the-scene dirt causes face cancer—the people they send to work in the access shaft don't matter to the Powers That Be. I empty my lungs of filthy working-class air and pull in Butterfly's clean, bright, upper-class freshness.

I want the door exactly like I found it, maybe half an inch shut. I'm easing it back into place when something near the floor catches my attention. It's a tiny paper strip, maybe two inches long, fluttering on the edge of the door.

As I push the door closed, it matches up to another strip, attached to the wall.

Opening the door, I tore the strip.

There's a little bulging white dot glued to the wall. I wouldn't have noticed it if it wasn't for the torn paper.

Paper with silver lines.

That isn't paper.

It's part of a circuit.

A circuit I broke opening the door.

The perps didn't wire the door to blow. They wired it with an alarm, to tell them if someone followed them.

From somewhere further in the building I hear the drumming of running feet, accompanied with a rhythm section of heavy gear clunking in time with each step.

I'm blown—not to the Embassy Building's security, but to the perps.

And they're pros.

7

I break into a run.

I've studied the city office blueprints of the Embassy Building, of course, paying special attention to the Butterfly Star floor. Blueprints don't tell you that they painted everything except the floor this annoying eggshell off-white.

My gray-green jumpsuit, dark hair, and green zebra face paint don't buy me any stealth at all in here. A spangly-white disco outfit would hide me better.

I pass a door labeled RAT LAB and catch a faint animal whiff, then veer through the glass-walled kitchen. Someone's left half a sheet cake on the counter, almost petrified after the long weekend, and the store-bought sweetness with a hint of rot fills the air. It takes me away from the computer room, but the limited information I have tells me that the perps are focused the computer room.

I need to come around the back way. Through the cubicle farm.

Scope out the opposition and figure out their plan.

Butterfly doesn't give their administrative staff cubicles, though. It's an open floor plan, long flat tables with an in-and-out box and a flat panel monitor on each, a cheap office chair pushed up hard against each table. Everything is exactly in its place. The fake pine smell is stronger here, with an underlying noxious whiff that twists my stomach. There's no outside window. Most of the tables have one little bit of decoration, like a small framed photo or a tiny trophy. I bet if I found the employee handbook, I'd find a line starting with "Staff are permitted one small personal item, not to exceed four by six inches…"

I can imagine more dehumanizing office environments, but only without the Emancipation Proclamation. The Butterfly owners are not only greedy and selfish, they're flat-out ruptured hemorrhoids.

Maybe the perps *are* a blowout team. Hired by the staff. That would be nice.

Once I get the data, that is.

I need to make a few adjustments to my gear. Stash the backpack. Get some eyes.

Distant running footsteps.

I drop to my knees. Loosen my pistol in its holster.

A raised voice, made indistinct by distance and architecture.

The footsteps recede.

I get to the edge of the office space, where a half-open door exposes a dark meeting room. I exchange some of the gear on my utility belt for items from the backpack's bottom compartment. The last thing I take out is a tiny gas mask. I don't care about the gas part, but I make my gear do triple duty whenever I can. And I was about to go straight into air thick enough to chew.

I stash the backpack inside a credenza. Then I'm on top of the credenza. I pop a two-foot-square fiberglass ceiling tile, grab the edge of the wall, and hoist myself into the overhead crawlspace.

Most of the walls inside modern office buildings don't go all the way up. Restroom walls do, as well as some secure offices, but generally, they go up about six inches above the suspended ceiling, leaving a good three feet of dead space. Once I'm in there, I ease the ceiling tile back into its frame and push down the edges, sealing myself in darkness.

Here's where I need the infra-red goggles. There's all kinds of network and phone cable run everywhere, not to mention aluminum and steel structural supports running every which way. If you're careful and balanced and use your brain you can crawl along the top of the walls. I don't dare crawl quickly—I'm a little over six feet tall, remember? If I hurry, the weight will shake the wall under me and tell anyone with a brain precisely where I am.

It's hot. It's so filthy the wiring shaft looks pristine. I'm already sweating, and the sweat's leaving tracks in the dust already sticking to my face.

But slow and steady, I can get through this whole building and nobody'll know where I am or what I see. I can sneak in and rob these Butterfly bastards blind.

I've crawled about ten feet when my phone buzzes.

No, my phone doesn't have a cocky ringtone. It vibrates. Always.

And no, I don't answer it. Not while I'm balanced atop an eight-inch-thick aluminum strut meant to support drywall. Even if I wanted to, I'd have to lift up the mask to answer, which means I'd suck in a lung full of dust and dirt and probably little bits of that awful fiberglass thread they make ceiling tiles out of.

If someone's calling to tell me I'm blown, they'll leave a message.

So I ignore the intermittent buzz as I climb another few yards towards the computer room.

Butterfly doesn't have one of these military-grade or life-sustaining datacenters, just a computer room with extra cooling and connections to a backup generator. The city plans claim it has a drop ceiling just like the rest of the office. I should be able to get eyes on the perps from there, see who I'm dealing with.

I wear this tiny remote unit on the inside of my left forearm. Some of my gear can feed information there. If I have my goggles set to night vision, it automatically cranks the contrast down to gray-on-black that's clear as a Times Square billboard on Saturday night. If certain people send me a text message, it pops up there in minuscule letters.

It's Rob Fender.

Crap.

I owe him.

And the text reads CALL ME ASAP.

My phone has an actual physical keyboard. I can't type out long messages or anything, but I can flip the cover open, tap BUSY and hit Send, then flip the case shut.

I haven't gone five more feet when Rob's reply comes.

PERFORMING ATLANTA BUTTERFLY?

8

My guts seem to drop out of me.

There's only one reason for Rob to use that phrase with me right now.

He's the opposition.

Rob been in the business longer than I've been alive. He's not as brainy as I am, but I'm smart enough to concede that experience plus a pretty good brain will outperform a less experienced superstar brain. He's not as good with his hands as he used to be, but he knows loyal hands to hire.

And he stays bought.

I won't say we're friends. We get along well, and we've gone out to celebrate with him after a few really successful gigs. And by celebrate, I mean he spent a week in the expensive part of Rio with me (and Deke), blowing a few thousand of a "performed beyond expectation" bonus.

But if a contract brought us into opposition, we'd stay in opposition until the contract ended. Which probably means ending one of us.

He'd made a courtesy call.

If he knew it was me, he probably knew I was alone. He was giving me the chance to quit with the Catwoman routine, get myself out of the way before he and his posse launched me out a window.

He'd be really unhappy about it afterwards. Probably have a drink in my honor next week and every New Year's.

But he wouldn't hesitate.

No gloating.

No apologies.

Rob respects me way too much to hesitate.

Even for half a second.

The stale crawlspace suddenly feels even hotter and more cramped. My pulse throbs in my temples, and a headache billows at the top of my head. The gas mask over my mouth and nose seem tighter, the space around my mouth less humid.

No need for me to answer that message.

He already knows the answer.

Rob's got a contract. That contract doesn't include "let Beaks rob the place."

The message didn't mean Rob had been given my name. He could have figured it out from evidence. I hadn't left many clues, of course, but absence of evidence is a kind of evidence. That little open-door detector might have had a camera, or he could have put one nearby. He might have gotten a real good look at my face when I bent down to check out the tear-snip sensor, green and black camouflage stripes over my olive skin and all. Plus a better look at my oversized rear when I turned to flee.

Yes, I want the Butterfly Star research data. I want to give it to the world.

But do I really want to go up against Rob "You'll Never Know You're Dead" Fender?

Feet tromp below me.

I freeze.

They pass through the wall I'm balanced on. There must be a door right in front of me. There's a thud. A clank. Someone swears under his breath. Three quick beeps, then a click. A man says "Device sixteen. Meeting room four prepped," not loudly, but not like he's afraid of being overheard.

The feet tromp back through the wall, pass my feet, and recede.

I wait for them to disappear, then lie belly-down on the filthy aluminum strut so I can use my right hand to tug at a fiberglass ceiling panel below.

The goggles transform this meeting room into shades of green, but I can still make out the oval meeting table of polished mahogany, and the glass-fronted wet bar and the eighty-inch video screen behind the head chair.

If all eighteen of the executive chairs had held executives, I would have been perfectly happy to see the brutal, ugly device plopped on the table. Seeing as we were down a bunch of bosses and plus one me, the blocks of explosive and the detonator didn't thrill me.

9

I can disarm a bomb. Radio detonator? No problem. You study the wiring for a couple minutes and pull the correct wire. It only takes a little bit of brains.

Well, okay, a lot of brains. An understanding of electronics. And explosives. You've got to reverse-engineer the wiring from first principles.

But still. I can do it.

But the flunky had said *device sixteen*. Implying that there were fifteen more like it. At least.

This was a blow-out job.

If all sixteen bombs were the same size as what I'd seen, they might take the top ten floors of the tower with them.

Time to run. Grab my backpack and get the hell out.

I waver for a moment.

Go up against Rob?

It's not like our goals were incompatible. He was here to blow the joint. I was here to steal two labeled hard drives from the computer room. I could do the theft and clear out, leaving him plenty of time.

But he'd never go for it. A blowout meant taking everything with it, including any hard drives and any witnesses.

I (*we!*) would never go for it either. Against the spirit of the deal. And when you charge our—*my* rates, you keep the spirit of the deal.

Smart thing to do was run.

But I couldn't make myself do it.

After Newcastle, after everything that had gone so horribly wrong that one horrible day last week, I need a win. I need to strike a blow for liberty and hope and life and joy.

Somebody has to pay for Deke, and I'll never find the people responsible.

So I scuttle along the top of the ceiling as fast as I dared.

The computer room is easy to find from above. All the network cables converge on that one area. I turn off the infra-red, slide a tile out, see nobody, and drop to the white linoleum floor below.

Four rows of glass-fronted computer cabinets run from one beige gypsum board wall to the other, like library shelves. And it is a library, sort of. The computers humming inside these cabinets hold more information than the whole Library of Congress. Bundles of thick blue cables rise from each cabinet into the ceiling, running into special rings cut into the fiberglass panels right next to the brilliant banks of fluorescent lights. A dedicated air conditioner wheezes in the corner. In the back, a set of double doors lead to the lobby, for moving cabinets and heavy machines into this room. They're rather fancy dark wood, in case they have to be open when an important bastard comes swaggering in from the elevator. A single, much plainer metal door on the side leads to the computer operations staff area. The smell of floor wax is so thick it paints my tongue, and the machines hum and growl loud enough that I'd have to raise my voice to talk.

The whole room's just… sterile.

I know that there's a lot of geeks like me that like to play with computers—no, I take that back. I like to play with the information in computers, I like the number-crunching and the experimenting that they empower. I know there's a lot of innocent geeks who like fiddling with the machines and how they hook together, but they're just mechanics. They're like the guys who rebuilt car engines in the 1950s. Tinkerers, with less grease and more carbs.

I couldn't imagine spending my life servicing the lifeless life in this room, rather than playing with everything they empowered.

No time.

The rows are lettered. Each cabinet is numbered. I find row C, then scuttle down to cabinet 8, one from the far end. Green and red LEDs glow behind brown-frosted glass. I didn't bring the Lock-Release, but I learned to pick better locks than these when I was eight. Blindfolded.

Hey, locks were the toughest puzzle I could find back then.

But cabinet C8 is already unlocked.

The door is barely latched.

My stomach twitches with nausea and just a hint of fear.

The whole cabinet is dedicated to shelves of hard drives, mounted vertically in little plastic cases, snug up against each other. I skim down the cabinet, and—yep.

The drives labeled C8-115 and C8-116 are missing, plastic case and all.

Rob's got them.

Steal the data. Torch the building. Claim the insurance, shut down. Claim more federal funds under another name. Lather, rinse, repeat.

I stand up and shut the door, frustrated anger churning in my guts.

There's no way I can get the drives now.

I've failed.

All I can do now is escape before the blowout.

Outside the door, something dings. An elevator.

A high, threadbare voice outside the double doors shouts "Security!"

I freeze.

There's the pop of a handgun.

One shot.

Silence.

A man's voice right beyond the door says "Dammit."

Footsteps.

My guts plunge.

He wants to move the body.

The doorknob rattles.

Turns.

10

The computer room is all bright lights and square corners.

You can describe me in many ways, but "square corners" isn't one of them. Anyone who Rob hired isn't going to back into the computer room. They'll come in and glance down each aisle, verifying that their initial sweep didn't miss a rat.

The linoleum is a little slippery, but my boots hold just about anything.

The man who steps in is only a little shorter than me. He's wearing a short-sleeve button-up shirt and dress slacks, but he's ripped off the blue tie and stuffed it into the pocket. With those biceps, he looks like a gorilla stuffed into a clown suit.

One of those biceps has a tattoo.

USMC.

Shit.

The sound of my feet catches his attention. He turns just as I crash into him.

Some people call Marines dumb. Usually dumb people with dumb opinions.

You get a Marine by taking a normal healthy man, running him within an inch of his life, and teaching him that he can take a lot more of a beating than he ever thought possible. The first time you get socked in the jaw it's a shock. The fiftieth time, you think *I've had better punches from my grandma* and move in for the kill.

My only hope is an immediate takedown.

I knock him into the wall, trying to smack his head against the fire extinguisher cabinet and stun him. He stumbles but gets his feet under him right away, veering us off target a critical inch so he smacks the drywall instead of the steel case.

Shit again.

We're at it.

I sidestep a punch and whirl to his side, launching an elbow at his nose in passing, but he turns his head and leans in to take it in the ear. He swings his arm to grab me, but I dance out of the way. He's stronger, I'm faster. Eventually I'll wear him out, but I don't have eventually, his radio is already squawking asking what the problem is, so I jab loosely folded fingers at his eyes and make him recoil and blink.

Not even the Marines teach you to strengthen your eyeballs.

He raises his hands up instinctively and takes a step back to get a bit of distance.

I dance back as well, reaching down with the step.

My weight has barely shifted when I draw my .38 and shoot him point blank over his heart, the silenced report like a loud cough.

The impact knocks him back – he's got a bulletproof vest beneath that shirt.

So I shoot him between the eyes.

No hesitation, this time.

I didn't want to kill him. I went for a blackout hold, then a knock to the head.

But there he is, dead. Limp on the floor in his button-up disguise and blue tattoos.

Just doing a job. While the rest of the team is handing out the fireworks, he's guarding the back.

Shooting a security guard.

He'd sworn after shooting the guard.

Guess he didn't want to kill anyone either.

That's enough. I've got to get out of here. Everything is about to go to hell, and I've killed a man without getting anything.

I take a step into the lobby and stop.

The reception area inside the elevator is decorated with more money than taste. The walls have rich paneling, with gold-framed black-and-white portraits along one wall. I recognize the founders and principal backers from the files I've studied, but they're not nearly so prettied-up in real life. A stylized blue-and-red-and-gold butterfly dominates the wall behind the curved receptionists' desk. A phone on the desk blinks with enough light-up buttons to launch the USS Enterprise—the aircraft carrier or the starship, whichever. Even the plush leather chairs are better than any piece of furniture owned by anyone I knew growing up.

The security guard lies face down in front of the elevator. His peaked cap has rolled off, exposing a ring of thin hair yellowed by age. Rich scarlet blood stains a growing circle in the plush white carpet. Dammit.

I hate it when old men security guards die. They should be retired. They should get an adequate pension so they don't have to do shit jobs like guarding rich assholes' stuff on the Fourth of July. This whole system needs to *burn*.

The electrical wire stripper sticking out of the canvas tool bag plopped in the middle of the floor catches my eye.

Could I be that lucky?

Yes—it's an explosives tool kit. I thought I recognized that Marine's other tats. And right on top of the bag, in a clear plastic box, is a detonator.

It's roughly the size of a bulky television remote control. There's a big red button with a separate plastic cover toggled over it. Nineteen lights shine a merry green on it. One shines red.

As I watch, it turns green.

Twenty devices, ready to go.

But better still—beneath the detonator…

Two hard drives, in plastic trays.

Labeled C8-115 and C8-116.

We stop long enough to scoop his thighs in one hand and latch our hands behind his back in a fireman's carry, then grind forward, shoulders burning.

We're nearly at the wall when a chain of small explosions shatters the night behind us. Someone found Bradley's abandoned pack. But they don't regret it. People more than a few yards away might regret it, but whoever open the pack regrets nothing.

"Wall," Rob says into his throat mike. He stops.

I stagger to a halt before we wishbone Jacka. *Right. The wounded plan.* Strain burns down my shoulders. My breath slams my parched throat. I ache to release Jacka's weight, to set him on the ground and move free, but I won't. I won't.

I will *not* leave him behind.

I will not betray Jacka.

Like Deke betrayed me. Us.

Like Deke destroyed me.

The laptop seems its own nova of heat and light against my spine.

"Check," Bradley says.

I close my burning eyes, panting. My shoulders involuntarily hunch.

Jacka groans with the motion.

Another dull boom.

I open my eyes.

The night vision goggles show a bright green but quickly fading blotch on the wall, a couple dozen yards off our path. Explosively heated bricks still tumble to the ground.

By the time we get to the breach, the innkeeper's rusty rattletrap minivan pulls up. Bradley hops out to yank the sliding door open. We heave Jacka into the back, I pull the door shut, and we're off into the secret night.

31

The minivan smells like the back of a decommissioned garbage truck. I'm exhausted, but Bradley's driving and Rob's even more done in than I am and Jacka's oozing on the back seat. Blood's seeping over tattered cloth and into exposed foam padding.

Jacka doesn't complain, though.

He doesn't say anything.

I snatch the big combat medical kit from under the bench seat, strip off my gore-drenched gloves, and get to work. Working by penlight clenched between my teeth, I strap a layer of bandages over Jacka's shoulder and tighten everything further. I want to know how badly Jacka's hurt, but I don't dare cut away his sodden shirt or the makeshift bandages duct-taped over them. His thin face is always pale, but now he's the color of bleached paper.

If Jacka lives long enough to get to a doctor, it'll be a miracle.

But that miracle demands a little help from me.

Fortunately, I'd spent a whole month under the tutelage of an emergency room physician who was short on cash and long on gambling debts.

I pull an IV kit out of the medical kit and rip it open.

The minivan turns a corner, its suspension creaking and bouncing with the motion. I spread my knees further, trying to brace myself and not drop any of the plastic bits in the IV kit.

When the minivan straightens, I swab the inside of Jacka's uninjured arm with an alcohol wipe. "Needle time."

Bradley lets the minivan glide to a halt.

The only light is the tiny LED flashlight chomped between my front teeth. I'm parched, but somehow my mouth is watering and the flashlight growing slick. I need two tries to hit the vein.

The second I say "Go," we're in motion down vacant two-lane roads.

I hang the bag of blood expander from the crudgy Jesus bar and let myself relax.

Everything that can be done, is done.

Jacka's filling the bench seat and Rob's riding shotgun—with a real shotgun. I sag and turn to sit cross-legged on the floor between Rob and Bradley. Jacka's blood soaks half my heavy camo shirt. People slurry from the armored thug has transformed the other half into a paper mache shell.

The minivan's carpet feels grimy and leprous. For just a moment, I consider unearthing my bloody gloves from beneath the used medical supplies, tools, and wrappers I flung into the door well. Instead, I put my hands in my lap and lean against the bench seat. Jacka's warmth feels good against my shoulder blades.

I escaped Noah's estate physically unscathed, but my muscles and joints hurt like I've been bludgeoned by a squad of Marines with maces. If lugging Jacka out of Noah's estate had exhausted me, poor Rob must be a wreck.

I burn to pull out my laptop and study the data we pulled from Noah's house. See exactly how Deke betrayed me. Dried gore cracks across my knuckles as my fingers twitch against imagined keys. But the laptop is behind the bench seat, buried in the pile of gear. I constantly fight not to talk, to shout, to scream.

When we hit Newcastle, it had been Deke's idea to have me go into the ceiling and watch the security cameras while everyone else went into the labs. Having a sentry had seemed a sensible, rational precaution. Had Deke given me that role to save my life? To protect me, when everyone else in the team was going to die?

He'd betrayed us. He'd betrayed *me*.

And he'd regret protecting me.

I need to relax, but the tension ricochets around my body like a pinball. Every time the minivan hits a little bump, the floor lurches and knocks me against a seat, or the floor, or just rattles my bones against each other.

Fuming helps nobody. Not even me. Instead, I try to clear my mind and focus on my breath, my heartbeat. Meditating forty-odd stories above the ground was easier, but minute by minute I hold myself together against Deke's shattering treachery.

The rest of the ride is in darkness. The only sounds are the groan of the minivan's neglected transmission and Jacka's lurching breath.

But when we reach the safe house half an hour later, Jacka's still breathing.

<h2 style="text-align:center">32</h2>

Inside the safe house, Rob cracks open a bottle of water, puts it in my hand, and sends me to get cleaned up. I drain the water, and to my surprise I can hardly keep my eyes open long enough to scrub away the blood. I leave the gore-soaked clothes heaped on the bathroom's tile floor and collapse naked under the sheets of the narrow hard bed.

Eventually, the afternoon sun streaming through the thin aluminum blinds covering the high narrow window tickles my eyelids and teases me awake. I've overslept, by far.

My first thought is of Rob handing me the bottle of water. *He drugged me. The bastard roofied me.*

I'm not as mad as I should be, though. Last night's revelations still absorb all my anger. When we hit the safe house I'd been awake for twenty-odd hours. So exhausted, any time I spent frittering with Noah's data would have been wasted.

My head feels weirdly hollow. My tongue tastes bitter with last night's disaster. My empty stomach mutters and when I work my jaw my parched lips crack.

At least I got all the blood off of me before falling over.

Jacka.

I sit up, letting the coarse bedsheet fall away. It's warm enough that my sudden motion and the thought of an injured teammate triggers just a touch of sweat.

The plain room holds only this narrow Ikea bed and a fourth-hand pressed wood dresser. A weak breeze squeezes through the finger-wide space in the window, rattling the dusty cheap blinds and sending dirt skittering across the tile floor. The bathroom door hangs open, exposing yesterday's blood-petrified clothes and the cloud of flies basking in their miasma.

The dresser drawers stick, but the contents are arranged by size—small in the top drawer all the way down to double and triple extra large in the bottom. No underwear—everything's been chosen to equip the widest possible array of people with the essentials of decency. I find a pair of drawstring red terrycloth shorts that hang loosely over my hips and a T-shirt tall enough to reach them, advertising a Lisbon music festival.

No shoes or sandals. I open my door and follow the sound of voices.

The living room might be best described as *rustic*, if only because I'm too polite to call it *primitive*. The rippled plaster walls have seen better decades, but someone meticulously patched the cracks and carefully painted them a flat intense white. Above ocean blue crown molding, the walls curve to flow into the textured ceiling. The tile floor is cool under my bare feet, but the breeze flowing through the shuttered windows tastes warm. The wooden furniture would be antique if it was in better repair.

The long padded couch looks like a veteran of three generations of healthy athletic children. Rob, sprawled across it, looks just as rough. His dark skin has a waxy sheen, his eyes fever bright. Somehow, after last night's mayhem and hurried departure, he's wearing crisp linen pants and a white button-up shirt with a thin brown string tie. The matching linen jacket hangs neatly folded over the arm of the couch.

Bradley's sitting cross-legged on the floor next to the open screen door, in comfortable-looking slacks and a Portugal souvenir T-shirt, upturned feet in tightly laced brilliant white sneakers that would probably reflect enough sunlight to stop global warming. She looks fully rested and ready to go.

"Beaks," Rob says. "How are you?"

"I'm okay," I say. "Considering that you slipped me a mickey."

"I feared it was necessary," Rob says.

Bradley says, "You were half crazy last night."

Her words feel like a slap. "I was fine. I didn't rant or anything."

"You were about to detonate," Rob says. "Understandably, of course. A night's sleep hasn't improved your situation, but it did improve your ability to make sensible decisions."

Rob might be right, but I'm not about to admit it. "How's Jacka?"

"He made it," Bradley says.

"Thanks to you," Rob says, pulling himself upright. He's moving slowly and deliberately. "A physician met us here right after you went to sleep. Without your treatment, Jacka would have bled out on the way here."

I shrug. "You would have done the same."

Rob gives a tiny smile. "Dragging poor Dominic back from the estate almost did me in. My personal physician is likely to strain himself yelling at me at my next checkup."

Bradley says, "You're exhausted. She's up, go get some sleep."

"I'll stand watch," I say. "No problem."

"Momentarily." Rob massages the bridge of his nose between thumb and forefinger, letting his eyes drift closed. He moves like every muscle drags a heavy chain behind it. "We should briefly discuss what we learned."

"You looked at the data," I say. My heart revs up a gear.

"Once I arranged for Jacka to receive medical care," Rob says. "And contracted a few local professionals for guard duty." Knowing Rob, those local professionals could be anything from off-duty police to Mafiosi. "And sent Bradley clothes shopping."

"I got you a few things," Bradley says, pointing at a bulging white plastic shopping bag the size of a stack of seat cushions.

I'm picky about my clothes, but whatever she's found has to be better than the castoffs I scrounged. "Thanks." If the bag includes underwear I'll even be grateful. I sink into a rocking chair opposite Rob's couch. I'm still a little groggy from the ten-hour nap, but anticipation tightens my shoulders.

The chair rocks too easily. I tense my legs a little to push it back and hold it still.

Rob opens his eyes and folds his hands in his lap. "Noah has property all over the world. He's heavily invested in biomedical research. Companies he owns appear to have created a variety of medical treatments."

I clench my jaw against impatience. Noah, yeah, I want to crush him, but what I really care about is Deke. How could he have turned on me? On our team? How could he have just walked away from me without a word?

But Rob knows what I need. He's going to explain what he discovered. I need to let him have the floor.

"It appears," Rob says, "that Noah's companies are fed research directions from his plantation in Myanmar, near the Chinese border. He has an extensive, cutting-edge research facility there. One that operates under less than ethical standards."

I say, "What *exactly* do you mean, 'less than ethical?'"

Bradley's studying her knuckles. She's heard this before. Who knows what they talked about as I slept? What plans they made?

"In the civilized world, medical processes are tested first on computers," Rob says. "The ones that look promising receive testing on a series of animals. The most promising of those processes then proceed to human trials. Noah has accelerated progress by abandoning animal trials and proceeding directly to human experiments. When his people find something, they send carefully sanitized data and suggestions to his more ethical businesses."

"Hang on," I say. "Yeah, that's horrible, but—it can't work that way. You'd go through lots of people."

"People are cheap," Bradley says. She's still studying her knuckles, like she doesn't want to pay attention to the words coming out of her mouth. "If you don't care where they come from or how they live, or how they're going to live after you're done with them. People are damn cheap."

"Especially when you can import them from China," Rob says.

"Okay," I say. "Okay." Noah's Myanmar site is horrible. "We need to take Noah down." My heart doesn't have space for that horror. "But…"

I can't make myself ask. My neck and head tremble. Tiny muscle spasms quiver up and down my back. The rocking chair tilts a little further back as my legs tighten.

"Deke is a guest at Noah's Myanmar compound," Rob says quietly. "He has a private cottage on the grounds."

My tongue feels thick and heavy. "Under guard?" Is—is there *any* chance that Deke is Noah's prisoner?

"Reports show regular deliveries to Deke's cottage," Rob says. "The meals are not prisoner fare. The wine isn't exemplary, but probably excellent for that part of the world. And yes, the compound has proper cells, in an extensive series of underground caves." Rob's voice picks up a thread of tightly restrained anger. "It's clear that most of the people in that facility don't want to be there."

My conflicting impulses clash. Noah's exactly the sort of rich exploitative jackass I love to burn. Using unwilling human beings as first-line research subjects is an appalling new low even among the people I target. There's a thread in me that wants to smash open that compound and free the people inside. To pillage every penny, every treasure, every bit of loot Noah's ever valued, and split it between his victims. It wouldn't nearly be enough, but when accompanied by Noah's severed head impaled on a pike, it would have to do.

But Deke's in there.

And I don't want Deke. I *need* him. I need to grab him by his shirt and scream at him. I need to know how he could turn on me. If I don't learn that, if I don't understand how the man I love—*loved*—so deeply and completely could betray me like that, I'll never trust another human being again.

They say to turn the other cheek.

But I was going to throw the other fist instead. And a kick. And probably half a pallet of plastic explosive.

My hands are clenching the hard edges of the rocking chair's wooden armrests, gouging lines into my palms. I unclamp my fingers and peel my hands off the pitted varnished wood. I wiggle my fingers to get some circulation back and fold my hands in my lap.

Bradley isn't studying her own hands any more. She's eyeing me nervously.

Rob's sitting straight on the couch, but his posture has just a little bit of exhausted sag. The only thing keeping him awake is willpower.

I know what I'm going to do. But I make myself slow down. Without Rob and Bradley, without Jacka, I couldn't have learned about Deke. I'm going to approach this like a grownup.

"You know I'm going after Deke," I say.

Rob nods. "And we're going after Noah's compound."

"We have to," Bradley says. "It's not like we have a choice."

"You could fade," I say.

Bradley shakes her head.

Rob says, "My sources inform me that another half-dozen freelance specialists have been murdered in the last twelve hours. It's impossible to say that Noah arranged them. But the deaths are consistent with the information Deke provided Noah."

"And if the bastard's killing any specialist he can find," Bradley says, "he's sure not going to let the people who blew up his favorite mansion skate."

So: it's Noah, or us.

Deke, or me.

I can live with that.

I'm going to have to. No matter how much it hurts.

33

A banana, a glass of milk, and an open-face peanut butter sandwich on thick fresh-baked brown bread with French apple jelly silence my gnawing gut. The clothes Bradley got me lack any sense of style, but that's kind of the point. And she got me underwear, right size and everything. They're bikinis, not my usual hiphuggers, but that's still a huge step up from going commando in third-hand shorts. I'm in tightly laced brilliant white sneakers and a drab white sundress when I slip into Jacka's room.

Jacka's room is a little larger than the closet where I slept, but not much. It's painted the same flat white as the rest of the place, but has a wood-framed faded photo of a family's idealized previous generation hanging next to the door and a tiny wooden crucifix of ancient shriveled wood mounted on the far wall. He has a better window, too, cracked to blow away the twin taints of antiseptic and injury. His narrow bed looks a little softer than mine, too.

But to look at Jacka, he's going to spend a lot of time in that bed.

Jacka always looks pale and thin, but now he's downright gaunt. His lips are shrunken. His skin is tight over his cheekbones, and his eyelids heavy with painkillers. The thin pajama pants hang on him like he's a clothes hanger, and the tidy but thick gauze bandage over his shoulder is only barely whiter than his skin. He's half-sitting, back propped on this heap of pillows stuffed between his back and the wall. His eyes are loosely focused on this little tablet when I come in, concentrating on the tinny conversation of an old movie or something, but as I close the door behind me he looks up. He fumbles three times to stop the video. "Beaks. How you doing?"

"Better than you," I say, trying to keep my voice upbeat and cheerful. I'm still angry at Deke, but I've managed to turn it down to a simmer on the back burner. You don't yell at a maimed teammate, especially for what isn't their fault.

"I get to sit on my ass. For the next week or two," he says. "I'm doing awwwe-some." He's talking slowly, his voice wobbling up and down. The doc must have filled him with dope all the way up to the eyeballs. That's okay—use the painkillers, or the pain kills. And gunshots are painful. "Few days from now, I'm goin' down. To the coast. Rent a condo. Sun and sand and, and sea. For me! Grab a seat."

There's only space for one chair, this narrow wood thing you might use to interrogate prisoners, wedged into a corner near Jacka's feet. I sit. "Rob said you wanted to see me."

"Yeah. You get him t'go to bed?"

"Only after he introduced me to the guards."

"Good guys?"

"They'll do." I'd seen worse than the half-dozen armed men taking shifts around this isolated little house. I hadn't checked their skills, of course, but if everything went really bad their gunshots and final screams would give us time to slip out the back.

"Cool." Jacka reaches for a glass on the bedside table, but his fingers can't quite get a grip. I hop to my feet and help him get the straw into his mouth. He takes a long drink of water, then releases the straw. "Thanks."

I put the glass back on the table, right next to a bottle of Dilaudid. "You're a lucky guy. I don't help just anyone with their drink."

He coughs. "Yeah, first prize in… the bullet lottery."

"It could happen to anyone."

"I had night vision," Jacka says. Bitterness seeps through the drugs. "I was looking wrong way. Didn't even see, the bastard. Right round the edge of the bulletproof vest."

"Rob says you'll be up and working again, in no time."

"Yeah." His eyes get distant. "Maybe I should take the, the… hint."

"That's the pain meds talking. Give it a while."

"Not the first time I been shot," Jacka says. "Not the, worst, either."

Oh, great, I think. *He's going to tell his saga.*

But when someone's hurt, you keep them company.

"Used to love food," Jacka says. "Eat anything I, could get down my throat. Best out of three. Fought my weight. Had body… builder arms though."

My surprise must have shown. Jacka had been thin since Deke introduced me to him, on our third gig together. These days, Jacka could give diet tips to skeletons.

"Yeah," Jacka says. "Hard to believe, innit? Empty hand, that was my thing. Not punching, though I did that too." He licks his lips. "Throws. Locks. Controls and come-alongs. Get behind someone, I'd get them to take a nap. Every time." His eyes leave my face to stare into the past. "I did a thousand falls once. In two hours. No stopping just, just." He starts to mime slapping a mat, but his hurt shoulder jerks him to a halt. I flinch in sympathetic pain. "Just down and up. Threw my partner between each fall. Back and forth. Knew two hundred and six—six! Different joint locks. Only quit cause I had a date."

His eyes return to me. "I had a girl then, too. Siobhan. Engaged. Before I got shot."

I don't have anything to say, so I nod.

"On the job. Thought the bodyguard was down. Took a bullet." Jacka slaps his bellybutton. "Right here." And he's looking into the past again. "Deke got me out, but that's not, not the worst bit." He rubs his stomach with his good hand. "Peritonitis. Lost a bunch of gut. They wouldn't let me keep it either. I wanted to make guitar." His good hand waves absently. "Strings. Guitar strings."

Jacka's not the only one looking into the past. I've always admired the really good martial artists, all lithe and strong but smooth. I can see a younger Jacka, hair still full of color, dancing and gliding between thrown punches, effortlessly answering each grab or a swing by throwing his attacker at the ground.

Then maimed. Sick. Crippled.

"Couldn't fall," Jacka says. "Any more. Abs won't take it. Can't take a punch. Can't practice without falling. Couldn't even teach. What was I gonna do? Work in an office?"

"That had to suck," I say honestly.

"Siobhan going sucked more," Jacka says.

"That bitch," I say reflexively. You don't bail on someone because they're sick.

"Not her fault." Jacka leans back and closes his eyes. "She tried. I'd given up."

Jacka falls silent. I sit for a moment, then have to throw words into the gap. "Still, this isn't so bad. You'll be back up."

"It was Deke," Jacka says. "That saved me."

Listening to Jacka, I'd managed to forget Deke. The anger, the shock of betrayal, floods back into me.

"He got me up. Got me to a shooting instructor. Taught me how to find things. I had contacts. Deke showed me to, to use them. Found out, I liked to drive hard. Pilot. Helicopters, too. Speedboats. Still can't eat—every bite, it hurts. Going through. Lucky I don't have a bag, though. Still can't take a punch. To the gut. But, I've got, a life. And Deke, Deke… he gave it to me."

Deke had never told me any of this. Like he'd told me many times, some stories aren't his to tell. I'm fighting tears again, struggling against this surge of blended sympathy and pride and rage at him.

There were good reasons I'd fallen so hard for Deke.

"Point is," Jacka says. "Point is, I owe Deke. So, I gotta ask."

All those emotions flash-freeze into a knot in my throat. *Don't you dare tell me what to do with Deke! Please, please ask me to save him, to kill him, to crucify him, to forgive him, to burn him.*

"When you find him," Jacka says. "You find him. Please." He heaves a deep breath. "Make it quick."

I'm trembling. The peanut butter sandwich has turned to acid in my stomach.

But I can't throw my anger in Jacka's face. Not right now. He got shot helping me.

It takes all my self-control to say, "I can do that."

Jacka pulls one eye open long enough to say, "Thanks."

We sit in silence for another moment. I'm trying to hide the emotional hurricane battering my soul. Finally, Jacka fumbles for the glass again, and I swoop in to help.

"You don't need to," he says when I put the glass down. "Sit here. Watch a sleeping man."

"I'll let you be," I say. "You rest."

My hand is on the doorknob when a sudden thought strikes me. "Jacka?"

He grunts, maneuvering himself to lie more flat.

"You—you only flirt with the attached women, don't you?"

The left side of his mouth quirks up. "It's fun. But can't have anyone… take me serious."

His words make me a little sad. Jacka's totally not my type, but I suddenly understand he isn't quite as obnoxious a guy as I'd thought. No—he's still obnoxious, but I can understand why.

And everyone deserves hope. Even for love.

I watch him wiggle down between the pillows to make himself comfortable. "Next time I need a driver," I say, "you're getting a call."

Jacka gives a drowsy nod.

After all, he was a good driver.

And he wasn't going to flirt with me. I wasn't attached to anyone. Not any more.

34

In a big wicker chair with a really thick cushion in the corner of the safe house's dining room I dive into the data we extracted from Noah's estate, and find myself forced to agree with Rob. Several messages mention Deke's private cottage in "the compound." One says that the locals had "assigned the ever-willing and *very* flexible Miss Xi to attend to Eckhart's most personal requirements."

Reading that, I throw myself out of the lopsided chair and march out to the safe house's tiny courtyard. It takes an hour of karate kata, each strike thrown brutally, before the red rage recedes enough that I can return to work.

Deke's leaked details on thirty-nine freelance specialists. Some, like Pillock and Daft, he's given safe house locations and phone numbers and the names of their Parisian haunts. Others only have a name and a contact method.

Bradley's not on the list. Or Jacka.

Weirdly, neither is Rob. Deke knows a lot about Rob, down to the computer codes to hook into Rob's private virtual network. There's nothing on the list, though.

I'm not on the list.

Because I have a whole separate file.

Deke hasn't just spilled everything about me professionally.

He's spilled *everything*.

Likes and dislikes. Favorite colors and outfits. Where I get knots in my back, and how I like them massaged out.

How to escalate that massage into more than a massage, and what I like him to do then.

89

With very… precise details.

My face burns with humiliation. My heart pounds. I want to set something on fire, but if I quit now I'll never return.

My dad's address.

And at the very bottom—my *mom's* address.

Mom split when I was ten. If she'd stuck around, she would have lost the few teeth she had left—unless Dad broke her neck first.

I'd looked for Mom. I'd searched, so I could either hug her or slap her. Probably both.

How had Deke found her?

And how long had Deke been holding that secret?

How long had he been waiting to use my mom against me?

Kata aren't enough this time. I grab Bradley for some flat-out sparring. At least, it's flat-out for me. Bradley sidesteps almost every strike, and I'm pretty sure she permits me the blows I do land.

Bradley doesn't ask why.

She's too professional to not read everything.

Dammit.

It's another hour and a half until I can bow out. Bradley thanks me for the warm-up. I take a shower and drag myself back to work.

Other messages hint that Noah is on his way to, or already in, this Myanmar compound. Deke's enough reason for me to go to Myanmar. But if Noah's there, if I can put Noah down like the maniac he is, that's gravy.

The sensible flight from Lisbon to Myanmar is Emirates Air, with layovers in Dubai and Singapore. Rob and Bradley get the easy route, but I'm not visiting the United Arab Emirates any time soon—I have three different death warrants there, under three different names. Seems the combination of theocratic royalty and ridiculous wealth brings out my worst nature. And the UAE has some of the best facial recognition software in the world. A false mustache and a haircut won't do.

I wind up with Air France from Lisbon to Paris, with only a one-hour layover to catch a bus to the hub and another bus to the other terminal. Charles de Galle airport has all the simplicity and elegance of five gallons of boiling spaghetti. Fortunately, the only luggage I have is this flimsy plastic satchel with my tablet and the rest of the clothes Bradley bought.

The stupidly long flight to Singapore, wedged in a middle seat between this sweaty chubby Chinese guy who desperately needs fresh deodorant and this Australian chick drinking enough to be noxious but not enough to pass out, gives me time to think. Time I rather wish I didn't have.

I love—*loved*—Deke. He'd saved me when my life fell apart. He'd helped me claim a new life. We'd been through too much to not trust each other completely.

But somehow, Noah had turned Deke.

When? When could this have happened?

How long had he been lying to me?

How much money does it take to destroy love?

I guess the answer is, "Little enough that Noah could write the check."

I felt desperate to believe that Deke was imprisoned. That he'd been captured, and that they were opening his brain with drugs or torture or wires to the brain. But nothing in the emails even implied that. And Noah's people had no problems putting appalling things in email. They had lost twenty people testing a possible new antibiotic derived from a newly discovered Tanzanian fungus. Another message mentioned that the compound had acquired another dozen subjects for a "head transplant research program" and that the surgeons were hopeful to achieve at least one success… this time.

Head transplants. How much would Noah charge one of his plutocrat friends for a whole new body? Someone young and healthy? The answer was almost certainly "less than some human monsters would pay."

Somehow, that doesn't anger me as much as Deke's betrayal.

I sit with the tablet on my lap, utterly unable to concentrate on the latest batch of comics. My headphones and Screaming Females on shuffle block out the airplane's roar and the hundreds of conversations around me. My legs are so long that I'm pretty much sitting diagonally, pressed up against the giggling Aussie woman, knees meeting the aromatic Chinese guy's. He keeps trying to get me too look at his face, but I avoid meeting his eye. Right now, my stare can knock someone dead.

Plus, I'm pretty sure that Air France pumps first class flatulence back to steerage. Because they can.

Eventually, I doze.

Singapore's airport makes more sense than Paris' Charles de Galle, but I have about six hours to go half a mile. Singapore's a transit hub, with crowds constantly flowing through the airport, so rather than risk being recognized I plop down a credit card for five hours of private silence in a tiny hotel room. The bed is as comfortable as a rocky beach and the shower hardly wider than my shoulders, but the air doesn't have even a trace of jet fuel or exhaust, so it's heavenly. My Jetstar Asia flight for the last leg is overbooked, and my legs still haven't forgiven me for the cramped flight from Paris, so I suck it up and buy the first class upgrade. One glare convinces the rich jackass next to me that he'd like to keep his hands to himself, and my knotted leg muscles gradually relax.

Thirty-three hours after leaving Lisbon, a smiling East Asian woman in a crisp uniform stamps my passport and welcomes me to Myanmar's capital, Naypyidaw.

35

Rob and Bradley rented a crumbling two-bedroom suite in this street-corner hotel in a town a dozen miles outside Naypyidaw, dating back to the colonial days when they called this country Burma. The dour British architecture has a fresh coat of fifteen different bright colors, like they got a discount on every color of paint the store couldn't sell. The whole country's that way, though—gaudy colors and ridiculously over-armed soldiers. You have to look more closely to realize that the colors and the spectacle cover decayed infrastructure. All of Myanmar's worn down to a prancing skeleton. Most of the building is trapped in the 1930s, with plumbing and electrical to match, but it's far from the tourist sites and the suite commands a view of the crossroads. There's no air conditioner, but a rickety ceiling fan stirs the sticky heat.

Bradley steers me to a thinly padded wicker chair built for a big Oriental guy. My hips barely squeeze between the chair's arms, and the bamboo frame creaks with my weight. But Rob's sitting on the bed, looking completely alien in touristy shorts and a T-shirt with yet another tablet on his lap, and Bradley's perched on this tiny folding chair.

My stomach rumbles at the smell of frying fish and hot peppers and all sorts of stir-fry vegetables squeezing through the cracked window. Naypyidaw street food smells fantastic. I knew one American who tried it. He loved it, raved about it, and six hours later got flown to a Hong Kong hospital to be fitted with a whole new microbiome.

But after that flight, I'm so tired that for half a second I consider a skewer of unnamed seafood in questionable spicy sauce just for the vacation.

Both Bradley and Rob look tired but ready for action. Thanks to Emirates Air, they've been here for nine hours.

"Beaks," Rob says. "Welcome to the party."

I really must do something about those UAE death warrants. "Call me fashionably late."

"Glad we could get everything ready for you," Bradley says with only a hint of sharpness.

"I appreciate it," I say. "What did I miss?"

Rob reaches over to a folding table by Bradley's chair and lifts a steaming china pot. "Tea?"

"No thanks." They say drinking hot tea cools you. I say they're crazy.

Rob lowers the pot. "Feel free to change your mind, it truly is excellent. Noah's spread a great deal of money around—by Myanmar standards, at least. My contacts have come up with the location of Noah's compound. The most recent satellite photos I can access are from May, and they're mediocre at best. Hopefully little has changed in two months."

"I've worked with worse," I say.

Bradley says nothing. I've missed their discussions, again. Voices in the back of my head mutter about secrets and fresh betrayals. But Rob and Bradley didn't maneuver for time alone. They didn't know about the UAE thing until I brought it up. Deke has ripped a hole in my soul, and it seems that everything everyone says and does wants to fit into the gap he tore.

They're not betraying me, I keep telling myself.

"My initial assessment is that we need a penetration team of four to five people," Rob says. "We should have a spotter and a sniper, plus a pilot for the extraction helicopter."

"How long until they get here?" I say.

"Never," Bradley says.

Surprised, I glance at her heavy face, then back at Rob.

"Another five freelancers have been killed since we left Portugal," Rob says. "The assassins are clearly corporate mercenaries. Word travels quickly. Most of our peers have gone into hiding."

"Deke didn't leak everyone," I say. "Surely people not on Deke's list—"

"Nobody but us has that list," Bradley says.

"So we tell them," I say.

"You would soil Deke's name on suspicions?" Rob says.

"Suspicions!" I fight to keep from shouting. "He turned. What is there to suspect?"

"We don't know the details," Rob says. "Noah might have leverage."

"What leverage?" I say. I'm holding my voice quiet, but my wicker chair creaks when I speak.

"Everyone has family," Bradley says. "What would you do if someone threatened your folks?"

Dad's too drunk to notice, and Mom, well—who knows? "Still, we have to warn them."

"I contacted everyone Deke exposed," Rob says. "Everyone is in hiding or unreachable. People are planning to strike back against the threat."

"Bring them here," I say.

"We must assume everyone Deke exposed is being actively pursued," Rob says. "If even one of Noah's targets is caught or killed on the way to Myanmar, it will alert Noah that we're moving against him."

"So call the second tier," I say. "Give, oh, Stabbity Joe a ring."

Bradley huffs. "Stabinowitz? Even that nutjob's in hiding."

"We do have some help," Rob says. "Myanmar is a delightfully corrupt country, even after the recent electoral changes. I've arranged transport to the village closest to the compound in a military transport. We leave early tomorrow morning. I have the name of a villager who speaks English and is willing to guide people to a lookout over the compound for a few dollars."

"Good," I say. "All we need now is a plan for three people."

Rob says, "We've had time to talk while you made your way here. And we have a… workable outline. Not ideal, certainly, but a perhaps viable script."

I feel a quick stab of jealousy at being left out of the planning—but what did I expect, that they'd sit here watching old movies? "Cool. Let's have it."

Rob says, "We want you to provide tactical support and sniper cover while Bradley and I go in to take Noah."

36

Everything seems to lurch to a halt.

The elderly colonial hotel room feels hotter and more claustrophobic. Walls thick with old beige paint press in on me. The smell of cooking seafood and vegetables and peppers from the crowded noisy street below turns rancid in my gut. Sitting on the bed, Rob suddenly looks like a pod person, a shabby alien duplicate in denim shorts and blue T-shirt instead of the real Rob's impeccable suit. Bradley watches me, deliberately relaxed but ready to throw her stocky frame at me if I lose it.

Which I just might.

Don't kill them. I work my jaw a moment as if trying to swallow the idea. "You want me. To wait outside. While you two go in to extract Noah?"

"That is correct," Rob says. He's sitting straight, like a commanding officer who doesn't even conceive the crew might mutiny. I've seen him worried, tense, even scared, but his dark face shows nothing but confidence.

I look over at Bradley.

She nods, once.

"Why?" I snap, lunging to my feet. I try not to shout, but my voice rises with my racing heart. "Deke is in there! Do you think I'm just going to sit by and let you two ignore that? Deke sold us out. Deke got people killed."

"You won't be sitting by. We need a sniper, a spotter," Rob says. My outburst doesn't unsettle him at all.

"While you go after Noah," I snarl. "Not Deke."

"Noah is killing our peers," Rob says. "Our friends."

"And Deke is feeding Noah all his information."

"Our first priority must be stopping the deaths," Rob says. "That means taking Noah."

Bradley's fidgeting on her undersized chair. Words want to burst out of her, but she keeps glancing between Rob and me. They talked about this, too, I realize. They agreed beforehand that Rob should do the talking, Rob should sweet-talk me into giving up on Deke.

"We stop the flow of information," I start—

—but Rob interrupts. "Noah is directing his own performance now. He is paying people to commit murder. We simply must call off those assassination squads before more people die."

"So we go in together," I shout. "The three of us. We can detour on the way to grab Deke."

"Three people extracting two?" Rob says. "Two *unwilling* people?"

"We, we steal a car," I say, but my voice falters at the end. It sounds weak, even to me.

"Without cover?" Rob asks. He sounds gentle again, like he thinks he's convinced me. "Through the jungle? Pursued by Noah's men?"

"You're the expert!" I say. "You've done this dozens of times. There's a way to do it, we only have to figure it out."

"I have done this," Rob says. "I've done this work since before you were born. Any script that calls for three people to extract two uncooperative targets from a fenced-in, heavily guarded compound deep in the Burmese jungle completely collapses in the second act. We do not have the equipment, the support, or the intel that would make such a thing possible."

Staring at Rob, I'm shaking. Deke helped me reassemble myself after everything I thought I knew had collapsed under me. And then he betrayed me, us, destroying my life again. I'm furious. I'm wounded. I'm crushed. And my soul still feels like it's exploding within me.

"This is an incredibly difficult performance," Rob says. "I know of nobody who has accomplished anything even remotely this chancy. Our very survival demands perfection. Professionalism. Detachment and dispassion. And you..." Rob shakes his head. "My dear Beaks." His voice is soft again. Tender. "You cannot be dispassionate now. Not even an ogre could expect that of you. Not now."

Dispassionate? Noah somehow turned Deke. If I see Noah, even through a sniper scope, I'm likely to put a bullet in him. If I have to smell him, he might just choke on my fist before I can say a word.

Rob's watching me calmly, trying to pull my focus onto him. It's an old trick, one I learned from him years ago. I deliberately look over at Bradley, who has shifted a little forward in apprehension or anticipation or both.

The gears in my brain feel jammed, immobile, so it must be my mouth speaking on its own. "Not a chance."

Rob starts to reply but I steamroller right over him. "You think I'm going to watch this through a sniper scope? I am going in there. I am finding Deke. I am dealing with him myself."

Rob says "I swear, we shall—"

"Nothing," I say. I'm not shouting now, I'm too mad for that. "You grab Noah—*we* grab Noah, and Deke will vanish. He will fade, right into the jungle, or over the border, into China, and then what?"

"He will show himself again," Rob says.

I'm on my feet. "Thirty days from now he'll have a new face. He won't even—*smell* the same." Deke's smell comes back to me suddenly, his own sweat mingled with expensive spicy cologne.

I might smell that once more. Just once.

"We'll never find him," I say. "Two months from now, he could walk right up to me and—and I wouldn't even *recognize* him. I have to find him *now*. Or never."

Bradley stands. "You selfish bitch."

I turn to her. Bradley's face is bright red, her teeth clenched.

Rob says "Liza, we agreed—"

"I agreed to let you try" she snaps, standing. "Good try." Bradley pivots to me. "People are getting killed out there, and all you can think about is your hurt feelings. You think you're the only one out there who's lost someone? Who's gotten backstabbed?" Her forefinger jabs in my direction. "That's what this business is all about, missy. We get hired—because *someone's betraying someone*. Only they can afford to have *us* do the betrayal for them, and pay again to have us clean up the mess so they don't have to face the person they betrayed."

I recoil. I'd never thought about my career in that way—it's always been about getting rich people to pay me to rob other rich people. But my brain's already overflowing. "I'm still going after Deke."

"Do you even know what you're going to do if you find him?" Bradley shouts. *Shoot him. Hug him.* "Get an answer."

"And what if you don't like the answer?" Bradley takes half a step towards me. "What if that asshole turns you too?"

That asshole can't turn me, and he's not an asshole! "He's not going to turn me."

"You've already thrown us over for him!" Bradley's so mad, her jaw shakes. "What would it take for you to forgive him? A crooked finger? Or just a big enough check?"

My hand lashes out. My open-hand fighting isn't very good, but this doesn't have any skill behind it. It's just a rage-backed slap.

Bradley ducks it, coming back up to shove my arm as I swing past her. It's textbook technique, and she's got a lot of strength in those brawny shoulders.

I stumble backwards, crashing into the hollow plaster wall. The whole building echoes with the impact and decades of dust rains down from the overpainted crown molding, but I bounce off the wall and find my balance almost instantly.

"Stop," Rob says.

I freeze.

Every time Rob's been involved in a gig, he's been in charge. I'm too accustomed to obeying him. My head throbs with rage, my hands clenched into tight fists just right for belting a self-righteous bitch.

But starting again means Rob will take Bradley's side. And Rob doesn't fight to subdue. He goes straight to breaking bones.

Bradley's still red-faced and has her arms raised before her face, but her hands are open. She's ready to defend.

I can feel Rob staring at me.

I don't take my gaze from Bradley.

"I happen to be the only one who knows where Noah's compound is," Rob says. His voice holds no emotion, at all. "Fortunately, I anticipated Miss Salton's decision." *Not Beaks. Not anymore.* "As she will not help us with the preferred script, we move to the second."

I take my eyes off Bradley to see Rob studying me. He's looking at me like I'm a hostage and he's debating if I can be trusted to take his list of demands out to the police.

"Second script?" Bradley says. "What's *this* plan?"

Rob says to me, "The second script gives Miss Bradley and I an excellent chance of extracting Noah. It also gives you excellent odds on reaching Deke, and the opportunity to suitably resolve your relationship." Sadness touches his eyes. "The biggest drawback, Miss Salton, is that you very likely will not survive."

I still ache to deck Bradley, but instead I choke back tangled anger and hurt.

Through clenched teeth I say, "Plan number two it is."

Safety tip: if a nation has to sign treaties with more than one of its own cities, don't vacation there.

If that same nation doesn't recognize the local government it signed the treaty with, that local government's army, or that army's rocket launchers? Never mind the methamphetamine trade. Run away.

We, of course, ran towards.

Ask Google how to get from Myanmar's capital, Naypyidaw, out to Pangkham, this little town snugged right up against the Chinese border, and it'll say "nope." It's a whole lot easier to go through China first, which for us would be a whole new box of stupid. The alternatives aren't so much roads as a series of gradually deteriorating water buffalo tracks.

The three of us spend the next day under the ratty canvas hoop tent in the back of a jungle-corroded Japanese truck. I make myself sort of cozy amidst recycled fruit cartons bulging with secondhand electronics. It's close, and hot, and muggy. We have bags of equipment, but it's a weird mix. Rob couldn't get what he wanted, but he did the best he could. The night vision goggles are mediocre, but the bulletproof vests are top of last year's line. The plastic explosive is almost old enough to be unstable. I can't help wincing every time a truck tire plunges into yet another hole, but we don't blow up.

Every half hour or so, the truck stops so Rob can have a quiet discussion with heavily armed soldiers in yet another uniform. Every stop I glimpse thicker foliage and steeper hills. As the hills climb towards mountains, I start seeing waterfalls—not itty bitty rapids, but "plunge off the cliff screaming" waterfalls. Money changes hands, and the truck groans onto an even worse route.

But the silence is even more uncomfortable than the joint-smashing ruts.

Bradley's clearly still mad, but settles for laying across the wooden bench up against the cab, head on her folded camo jacket, trying to rest through the truck's lurches. She won't look at me.

I don't get it. Bradley's never quite liked me. Yeah, I yelled at her and tried to slap her, but she put me down solid. The plan is rough on me, but it gives Bradley and Rob a better chance of getting out alive than having me act as sniper-spotter.

Fine. Whatever.

Rob's attitude has changed, too. Intermittently, we talk of old times and old adventures. We laugh at failures and glory in successes. It's a past-centered conversation, for old people. Talk for people who don't have a future.

Because I probably don't have one.

And Rob wants to remember me kindly.

The plan is simple, like any good plan. We get to the village near Noah's compound and scout. At midnight I enter first, leaving a heap of mayhem at my entrance point and a couple places along the way. I use the noise as cover for finding Deke. Rob and Bradley use the mayhem to cover their own incursion.

Noah's thugs focus on me.

Bradley and Rob focus on Noah.

My natural cockiness tells me I'll make it out, that however many thugs Noah keeps they won't be able to catch me. There's this uneasy murmur of fear in the back of my head, though. Stealth is my biggest incursion tool. Deliberately making a ruckus isn't natural for me. It feels wrong.

Which it is. Every freelancer who tries playing Rambo gets killed or taken. Quickly.

Which is why Rob and Bradley haven't shared the extraction plan with me. They'll give me the chance to join their escape, if I live long enough to find Deke and rejoin them.

The breeze through the gaps in the canvas carries nasty tropical bugs and occasional currents of noxious smoke. I know we're getting close to Pangkham when the road gets so narrow that branches and leaves continuously brush against the canvas. At one point the truck plunges into a river crossing, sending water glooshing up through the gaps in the rotting truck bed. Our big duffel bags of equipment are waterproof, but a splash of nasty muddy water crests over the top of my boot and oozes down my sock.

I'll have to check my foot for parasites.

The water's barely gone when Rob hands out steamed pork-and-vegetable buns wrapped in wax paper. They're from the hotel kitchen, and should be safe for our delicate dispositions.

Late in the afternoon, the road switches from ragged to rumbly. Bricks. We take a couple of sharp turns, then the brakes squeal arthritically and we rock to a quick stop.

The engine shuts off.

"Stay here," Rob says. He flings the canvas over the tailgate aside long enough to hop down, then leaves Bradley and I in the dim still festering mugginess. Bradley rolls to a sitting position and stretches out her legs and arms. My sweat glues my clothes to me, and my butt feels like I just spent eight hours on a mechanical bull, but the canvas roof isn't quite tall enough for me to stand and stretch.

Heavy footsteps outside.

I reach to my belt for the .32 semi-auto.

"It's me." Rob flings the canvas open again, but this time clips it to the side. "Come on."

I squint against the brain-piercing brilliance of the tropical sunlight, then drag my heavy duffel and my aching bones out of the truck and into the brick-walled courtyard behind a warehouse. A knock-off Jeep sits a dozen yards away. Rob's talking to a pug-faced Chinese guy behind the wheel.

The driver can barely keep from sneering at Bradley and I as we heave and lug the duffels to the back of the truck. I itch to tell him that automatic weapons, rocket launchers, and explosives are not light. I hold my tongue. Bradley disdains to even notice him.

I heave the bag up and tie one end of the woven plastic strap to a convenient eye-bolt on the back of the Jeep. I'll have to go over by Bradley to tie the other end down.

"Here," Bradley says, holding her raised hands open.

So she *is* talking to me. Just for the job, but still.

I toss the end across to her.

Rob claims shotgun—that's his role as a man in this sexual-equality-forsaken part of the world. Bradley and I get the back seat. I'm behind the driver, which is where I'd rather be. I can put two rounds into his back before he knows anything happened.

Then we're wheeling out of Pangkham's surprisingly clean streets and into the jungle. The trees don't look that different from home—they're not maples and pines, sure, but they're not the thick vine-choked jungle full of tigers and lions like you'd expect. It's all wildly overgrown, though—Myanmar doesn't have a real winter, so the growing season is "always." I'm sure trying to hike through these hills would demand a machete. Or a chainsaw. After a day trapped in a canvas steam-box, though, I'm relieved to look out and see sky flashes between crowded leafy boughs. The mountains remind me of the Appalachians—too old and worn-out, slump-shouldered as if from centuries of human conflict. There's not a road as much as a rutted muddy path between the trees, a line of grass and truncated pencil-thin saplings marking the gap between the tires, going along the sides of hills and over the saddles between exhausted peaks.

The pseudo-Jeep's engine is higher pitched than the truck's, but louder. Without a roof or even canvas, the wind surges enough to make even casual conversation impossible. Everything stinks of faulty exhaust.

I don't feel like talking anyway, instead concentrating on the job ahead.

I'll escape Noah's compound.

I *will.*

The sun is nearly down when the truck stops on the upslope of yet another mountain pass. The sudden silence stuns my ears. "Village," the driver says to Rob. His Chinese-accented voice sounds strangely flat to my stunned ears. "Over hill."

"Then take us over the hill," Rob says.

"I not show face there."

Rob grimaces. "Fine." He hops down to the dirt road. "Wait here."

The driver doesn't even nod.

I grab the roll bar and pull myself up to stretch my legs. It also lets me watch the driver's hands and feet more easily.

He doesn't reach towards the gearshift. Or put his foot on the accelerator.

I feel kind of disappointed.

Rob trudges the couple hundred yards to the crest of the saddle. He looks for a moment, then starts back towards us. I spend the wait studying the thick forest around us, watching everything slowly shift in the breeze. "Good," he says. "Remember—I've paid you for a two-way trip." He raises a hand. "You see them on your next trip, you give them a ride back to Pangkham."

The man shrugs. "They ride."

Bradley and I unstrap the two duffels, releasing the driver to back a yard into the jungle for his bootlegger reverse.

Once the jungle swallows the jeep's roar, we hoist the duffel bags and march up the road towards Deke.

We crest the hill as quickly as we can, to minimize our silhouettes. But we're maybe ten feet down the other side when we realize something is very, very wrong.

38

The village sprawls across the grassy hillside, tumbling towards the flood plain below. Rob's pixelated low-res satellite photos said that Noah's facility occupied the opposite hill, separated from the village by an unbridged river, but it's hard to see that way with the sun in my eyes. A decrepit horse trailer, sides streaked with rain-driven rust, slouches on the near edge of town, its wheels bludgeoned off and the chassis leveled with chunks of wood. No electrical lines, no phone lines. The steady breeze carries the smells of manure and old smoke.

But there's no new smoke.

Even in this heat, people need cooking fires. One of these twenty or thirty ramshackle shacks should have at least a sputter of smoke for the wind to shred. Coming over the hill, I should have seen people walking or animals moving.

"No crying babies," Bradley says.

Rob holds up a hand. We stop, our shoes skidding on the dusty two-track path.

The flood plain is a shifting sea of green shoots. A dark shape moves near the river—a water buffalo, shrunk by distance.

"No music, either." These days, even remote mountain villages right next to China have a solar panel and a few third-hand iPods, gifts and hand-me-downs from boys gone to soldier.

I raise my hand to shield my eyes from the sun over the far mountain. Even with sunglasses, my eyes water. The two tracks veer towards a dilapidated stake truck parked behind the largest hut. Back home, I would have guessed that accumulating that much rust and corrosion on a truck would take thirty years of hard use. Here, in this wet steamy morass, maybe five. But the hood's closed, and the tires well-inflated.

This didn't look like a place where every family had a car. And the tire tracks go right there. If the villagers drove away, they would have loaded up that truck. So they'd gone by foot.

With my hand shading my eyes, though, I can peer across the river.

Noah doesn't have a facility over there.

He has a whole damn compound, a complex, growing up the far side of the valley.

It's far enough away that individual people dissolve into the distance, but my watery eyes can make a central metal building the size of a private aircraft hangar. Smaller buildings surround it, each with the blocky shapes of lumber or brick or metal. There's irregular shapes of bamboo construction scattered everywhere around them. A minuscule moving dot is a car or truck. There's a good couple hundred yards between the outermost buildings and the encircling guard stations—a kill zone. Probably a fence we can't see from here.

This isn't a village. It's the gatehouse to the compound.

Deke's somewhere in that compound, in a "private cottage." Which buildings are the cottages?

I'll have to stop someone and ask. Politely.

But coming to the village before hitting the compound was probably a mistake. Noah's compound is bigger than the village. It looms over us. I have no idea how they built something so massive out in the middle of nowhere, right next to the Chinese. The villagers would have run screaming to Noah the second they saw us… except they're already gone.

Bradley says, "Could Noah's men have just scooped up the whole village?"

"Perhaps," Rob says. Fresh sweat dots his dark face, and his eyes flicker everywhere. "Back up to the tree line."

Rob's right. I want to explain the missing villagers, but that's not our mission right now. It might be important—it probably *is* important—but the village isn't the safe landing point we thought it would be. Once you start exploring interesting detours, the whole mission falls apart. Bradley and I start humping the duffels back towards the trees by the peak of the road.

I'm breathing heavily, and the weight of my equipment wrenches at my shoulders and squeezes old sweat from my cotton shirt. Once we get in the trees, though, I'll get to drop the bag. Stretch my back.

We'd even scheduled time for everyone to have a nap. In rotation, of course.

Halfway back up the hill, Bradley huffs and trips. Her bag clanks into the dirt. She topples forward, catching her weight on her free hand to keep from face-planting straight into the dirt.

"You okay?" I say.

"Shit," Bradley hisses angrily. "Get it out, get it out!"

There's something sticking out of her left buttock. I need a moment to recognize it as a dart.

I pivot aside, looking back towards the village.

Something bolts through the air where I'd been standing.

I jump aside, hand scrabbling for my holstered pistol. "Incoming!"

Rob's already rolling away from me, coming up with his own .38 semiauto held in both hands. His head swivels from one side to the other, not back and forth, but absorbing the hillside and the village and everything in a single pass.

Then he's pulling the trigger, aiming down into the village.

I squint into the sun, and catch a hint of motion between the shriveled bamboo rods making up the wall of the closest hut.

It's a dark metal gun barrel, turning to catch Rob.

My semi-auto's plastic grip is sticky and clammy as I bring it up. I line up the sights and put a bullet through the hut, right below the gleam. A second bullet goes a foot to the left, a third a foot to the right.

A scream shatters the quiet.

The sniper's gun barrel jerks, then dangles skyward.

I scuttle to Bradley. She's lying on the grass, cheek pressed to the earth, twitching. The one visible eye judders in its socket.

I yank the dart out of her butt. "We got you," I say quietly. We'll have to drag her up the hill, figure out what was in the dart, and get a counter-agent into her. Then try to get out of here.

We're blown. We're totally blown.

And they want us alive.

That's really, really bad.

Time to run.

"Rob," I say. "Give me a hand?"

But Rob's down too, sprawled on his side like a discombobulated doll.

Rob was shooting at the sniper even before I was. How had he been hit?

I'm missing something.

But the answer is obvious.

That guy in the hut wasn't the only sniper.

A sudden stabbing pain right below the ribcage—not from the direction of the village, but from uphill.

From the trees we just walked through.

I seize the red-fletched dart that's sprouted from my abdomen and yank it free. What kind of drug is it? How much time do I have?

Up at the top of the hill, in the jungle! He's getting off his belly and standing. Camouflage doesn't help when you raise your rifle above your head.

My mouth tastes like garlic. That's a side effect of sodium thiopental. I'll be unconscious in thirty seconds. Fall over a lot before that.

No way out.

I drag my heavy pistol up. My fingers are clumsy, I have to squeeze tight to keep the weapon from squirting out of my hand.

Seconds to go.

If I let Noah's men take us alive, we die ugly.

The half of Rob's face I can see looks peaceful.

I can save him a lot of pain.

It's the kind thing to do.

I could jam the barrel under my own chin after.

Deny Noah something.

Deny Deke.

One last bloody shriek of rage at the world.

Instead, I wrench the .38 up towards the hilltop sniper and start pulling the trigger. The pistol jerks and wrenches in my hands, trying to bolt from my grip, but each time I haul it back, each shot more difficult than the one before.

There's another stab of pain, in my shoulder.

Another dart.

The sniper drops to the ground.

Did I hit him?

I keep shooting.

Furious screams from my mouth.

The gun clicks.

Empty.

Even without the bullets, it's too heavy to hold.

My hands, too far away.

My head, too.

The gun topples to the dirt.

Smell of garlic buries the stink of gunfire.

My heart sounds ponderous. Labored.

How much thiopental did they use?

Two darts.

One right by my heart.

Might never wake up.

My last thought is of Deke's big smile against the warm waters of Rio de Janeiro.

Then the crunchy brittle grass rolls up and swallows me.

39

I still taste garlic.

But old, metallic, crusty blood's in there too.

Bitter, aged puke.

Cold hard floor under my cheek. Concrete?

Dirt. Cold clammy damp hard-packed dirt.

It's under the rest of me, too.

I'm naked. Filthy.

It's hard to care.

Complete silence presses against my ears. My heart is thunderous, my breath a hurricane. And each breath digs a dagger-tip into my flank.

The unexpected *plonk* of a drop of water.

A rounded stone, pressing against my gut.

Assembling myself takes just about long enough to successfully press criminal charges against a billionaire. I find one hand and drag it through the dirt towards my face, then go to find the other hand, only to find that the first hand has vanished. The bruised knee sending its aches up to my shattered mind, complaining about the sharp corner of stone digging into it. I eventually figure out how to move my thigh and relieve the pressure.

A cold weight around my ankle. Both ankles. Digging into my instep.

But I slowly manage to drag my eyelids open and see the tight small rocky ceiling above me.

I'm in a cave. Not the sort of polished, snazzy cave that pigopolist Neanderthals would claim. It's all lumpy, everywhere. The only reason there's a floor is the dirt between lumps of rock. Gritty lime stains on the walls underlie the slow drip of condensation. The thiopental is wearing off—the garlic taste still seasons everything, but behind it is the cave's mustiness, like a refrigerator that hasn't been cleaned in months. This place has all the fresh air of a coffin.

To one side, a naked incandescent bulb forms a single point of painful illumination.

I'm cold. Shivering. My body feels clumsy, like it belongs to someone else, and responds only grudgingly.

And yes, I'm naked on the clammy dirt. I try to tuck my hands under my armpits, but a jerk around my wrists stops me.

Handcuffs. Old ones.

I could probably pick these with a plastic comb.

Which I don't have.

I try to pull my knees up to my chest for warmth. Something rattles as I move. Then something else jabs the top of my feet, pulling me short.

Manacles.

The heavy iron bands are attached together by a grungy metal chain, maybe a couple feet long. The chain is padlocked to another short chain, welded to an even grungier iron ring set in the wall.

Taken alive. This was all kinds of bad.

Maybe I would talk to Deke again.

And maybe I'd wrap that chain around his neck.

But beneath that flash of defiance, I feel weak. Exhausted. I must ration even my bravado, because once that's gone I have… nothing.

And we're here because of me.

I groan. My brain shouts at me to be quiet, but the thiopental muffles my thoughts.

The stage whisper is hoarse. "Beaks?"

I work my mouth, trying to put a name to the voice. "Bradley?"

"Yeah."

I inhale to speak, and the side of my chest jabs again. "You okay?"

"Rob, too." Bradley drops her voice even further. My ears struggle to sieve her words from the cave's silence. "I think I'm between you both."

I'm parched—another side effect. I shift to pull my butt closer to the ring in the wall so I can curl up for warmth. My brainstem's still running the show. I know I should kick myself into thinking, but that engine just won't turn over yet. I'm still an animal scrabbling for shelter.

But slowly, my eyes start to work.

I'm chained in a ragged natural alcove, just wide enough for me to lie down in, off of a gently sloping tunnel. The overhead light is out in the tunnel, to the uphill side, strung on a line of Romex stapled to the ceiling. I don't have a toilet, or even a hole in the floor—that weak trickle oozing down the tunnel's natural gutter probably isn't only water.

That pain in the side of my head isn't from the drugs, though. My fingers probe the bruised, pulpy flesh over my cheekbone, but a flash of pain through my skull repels them. There's another tenderness in the right side of my chest—broken ribs?

Some bastard kicked a lady while she was down.

So thirsty. Bradley's talking, but I can't focus enough to put her words together. I face away from the painfully exposed lightbulb and try to get my brain to function.

Raped? No, no extra tenderness down there. Or behind. That's something, I guess.

Light flashes against the wall.

Plonk.

A drop of water, falling from somewhere.

I can't think well enough to plan—but my brain seizes onto a little nub of rock on the back wall, about four feet up. It's shimmering, just a little.

I reach up with an outstretched finger to touch it, and the shimmer collapses.

My fingertip isn't just filthy with dirt now—the tip is muddy.

Water. Condensing on the walls, trickling down.

The dirt on my hands would absorb any moisture before I could get it off, so I lurch to my feet and slurp directly at the rock. The water's thin and tastes of lime and minerals, it's even harder than the water in the little Michigan farm town where we lived until Mom bailed, but it hits my tongue like distilled life, breaking up the copper taint of blood, and suddenly I'm crazy insane for water, suckling off the walls, lapping at outcroppings, thinking of nothing but how excruciatingly slowly the burn at the back of my throat eases.

You can lick an amazing amount of water off of the wall of a cool humid cave.

I'm not sated—not really. But I suddenly feel embarrassed for suckling from the walls.

No, not embarrassed.

Humiliated.

I've never been caught before. Let alone been knocked out, stripped, beaten, and chained up, the last three not necessarily in that order. For half a second I thought it could have been worse, but that thought drowns in the outrage welling up from my guts.

Someone is going to pay for this.

Certainly me.

But I'm not paying the bill alone.

40

"Beaks," Bradley says.

I'm on my feet, handcuffed hands pressed against the bumpy cave wall for balance. The thiopental puts this little spin on the world, but water clears the worst of it from my thoughts. The exposed light bulb out in the hall casts spears of painful light through my eyes.

I'm together enough to feel not only cold, but chilled. I'm simultaneously embarrassed at my nakedness, glad nobody can see me, and wishing Bradley and Rob were chained up with me, rather than just out of sight.

At least they'd be warm.

The clammy, still air seems like it's been in here at least since the 1950s. The lime smell is strongest, but beneath that there's waste and old blood and darker, ranker scents. I can only think that it's what decades of human suffering smells like.

"Beaks!" Bradley's abandoned the whisper, and sounds like she's about to escalate to shouting.

"I'm here," I say.

"What is wrong with you?"

I work my lips. The coppery taste of blood is gone, but the thiopental garlic still coats my tongue. I'll be tasting garlic for days. "Two darts," I say softly. "They hit me with two darts."

"Damn, woman, you're lucky to be alive."

Someone further away murmurs.

Bradley says "They hit her with two darts."

Another murmur.

"Rob wants to know, can you stand?"

I take one hand off the wall. The cave wobbles, and I keep the other on its outcropping. "Mostly. The chains are a problem."

"Are you hurt?"

"Busted ribs," I say. I turn my neck to try to work the aches out.

"The water should help," Bradley stage-whispers.

"I've already licked the walls clean."

Bradley pauses. "They didn't give you water?"

"You *got* water?"

"Bucket of water and an MRE. Both of us."

"You got the penthouse suite, Bradley."

There's another distant murmur.

"She doesn't have water."

"Or food," I say.

"Rob says, make sure you at least get some cloth between the manacles and your skin. You don't need blood poisoning on top of it."

Now I'm pissed. "You even got *clothes*?"

Bradley stops. "Beaks. What, exactly, do you have with you? Everything."

I grit my teeth. "Handcuffs. Chains on my ankles. Two hands to preserve the feminine mysteries. No food, water, or clothes, let alone a toilet. And you'd best hope you're uphill of me, because that last one's going to be important real soon now." It wasn't, not urgently anyway, but saying it released a fraction of my frustration.

"Rob and I got our clothes, at least. Well, pants and shirts. You must have really torqued them off."

"Good," I say. That was a little loud. If Rob raised his voice I'd be able to hear him, but no need to make anything easier for our eavesdroppers. I lower my voice but add intensity. "Because they're pissing me off something fierce."

"You know the best way to work out anger issues?" Bradley says.

"Robbing them blind."

"Try strangling the bastard with your bare hands."

I cough a laugh.

Bradley says, "Works for me. Every single time."

Another murmur.

"Rob says to encourage you. Tell you we'll get out."

"Oh, we will fucking well get out of here."

Another murmur. "He also says he's got a job for you."

My laugh this time is bitter. "Don't worry, I'm gnawing on the chain."

"No," Bradley says. She's exasperated, but she's still keeping her voice down. "He says he needs you to argue."

"What do you want to argue about?"

"Not me," Bradley whispers. "When someone shows. The more they talk, the more they reveal. And he says that you're the best one for that."

"Is he calling me mouthy?"

"He didn't say that. You did."

"Fine," I whisper. "Noah shows up, I'll argue with the capitalist pig."

Bradley repeats my words. "Rob says that's exactly the script he wants. See how far your chain stretches."

I should have thought of that—the thiopental is mud beneath my mind's tires.

If I pull my chains to their full reach of a foot and a half, lay face-down on the clammy dirt, and scooch forward until the manacles dig savage gouges into my feet and ankles, I can just get the top of my head out into the tunnel.

But it's far enough to see, a little.

The natural tunnel's maybe four feet wide, plus or minus a foot depending on where exactly you are, undulating vaguely upwards in one direction and down in the other. It's the sort of cramped, ancient place where you'd expect to find Christians desperately hiding from Roman soldiers. The floor is irregular stone patches interspersed with hard-packed dirt that retains the broken impressions of countless jagged high-traction boot treads. A gutter, carved by thousands of years of condensation, meanders down the center.

The human fittings feel old as well. Lime and corrosion covers the massive staples holding the power cable to the ceiling. The plastic sheath on that power cable was once white, but age turned it brown and flaky. The rusty light fixtures have heavy bases and broad cages of corroded steel to surround the bulbs, like something from a World War Two bunker. This might be a colonial British facility, or perhaps a rebel-run prison from the 1950s.

This décor lowers my opinion of Noah even further. If you're a sociopathic plutocratic billionaire with your own evil lair, for decency's sake—update the fixtures in your prison. I'd be ashamed to lock up good guys in this pit.

There's no sign of surveillance, but it's best to assume it's there—that's why we're whispering.

I'm quietly describing the corridor to Bradley when movement catches my attention.

Uphill, on the far side of the tunnel, just above the floor, two hands thrust out into the hall and wave.

"That you, Bradley?" I stage-whisper, just as she says "Can you see me?"

I give her a moment to answer, then say "Yeah. Opposite side of the tunnel. Maybe ten feet up."

"Cool," she says. "Can you reach across the tunnel?"

I lay flat and stretch my hands out, handcuff chain rattling between them. "Not quite," I say, gasping as my rib grinds. That's not a bruise, it's got to be broken. "About halfway."

"Damn." Bradley's hands disappear. "Stay there."

I relax and shift, trying to ease the pressure on my rib. Maybe I broke more than one?

It's about a minute later when Bradley says, "Okay, heads up."

Bradley's stretched her arms a little further into the tunnel. She's clenching a knotted wad of cloth in a fist. "Don't let this go past," she says.

She flings.

The twisted cloth ball sails through the air, climbing only because the tunnel floor drops away. It hits the dirt a few feet uphill, bounces off the wall, and rolls a couple more feet before coming to a stop.

"Got it?" Bradley says.

"Hang on."

Stretching, grinding myself into the dirt, I can just get two fingers around an edge of the cloth. The manacles are murdering my ankles.

"Well?" Bradley says.

"Working—" I gasp. Rocks dig into my gut, my breasts, my thighs. "—on it."

A millimeter at a time, I tug it close enough to get a hand around the cloth.

Untying the loose knot, it's a man's T-shirt. Size double-extra-large. Cave dirt soaking the back and stinking of Bradley's sweat.

It's the best thing I've seen since waking up.

"You've stopped huffing," Bradley says.

"I got it," I whisper. I know I can't be completely dehydrated; a tear flickers in the corner of my eye. "Thanks, Bradley."

"No problem," she says. "Really, I'm watching out for Rob. Seeing a real live naked lady might make him reconsider everything. That'd be terrible after a lifetime of hogging all the pretty men."

There's a murmur from further up the hall. Imagining Rob's genteel indignation makes me smile. Dammit, am I so low that a dirty T-shirt and a bit of teasing can raise my spirits?

Guess I am.

"Don't go to the party yet," Bradley says. "The real prize is coming."

I stretch out again, letting the tunnel's cold stone floor leech my little warmth from my cheek and torso.

Bradley waves a dull silver packet. "You ready?"

My mouth waters. I don't know what that packet is, but I know where it came from. It's part of an MRE, a military meal. It's large enough to hold a dried apple. Mashed potatoes. Maybe cookies. "Ready," I say.

The packet sails through the air. Unlike the shirt, though, the foil gives it a little extra lift. A little more resistance. It catches the air, turns aside, and plunges straight down to the floor precisely between our cells.

I twist and stretch. The manacles dig into my feet, my heels, scraping off skin and gouging at bone. I crush myself against the corner between my cell and the tunnel, panting, letting the broken rib savage me as I strain.

The sight of the packet sets my previously quiet stomach growling.

I strain harder.

Use the shirt as a flail, trying to drag it closer.

But even then, the packet's a good two feet out of my reach.

Finally I fall back, gasping.

Bradley says quietly, "I missed."

"Not your fault," I gasp. "Thanks for trying." I'm afraid to ask. "What was it?"

"Brownie," Bradley says. "The last thing left, sorry. I was saving it."

"We get out of here," I say, "brownies are on me. Hell, I'll *bake* them for you."

I am *not* going to cry. We'd argued, we'd fought, we'd splintered apart, and now Bradley has given me the shirt off her back and the last of her food.

Bradley says, "I like pecans in mine."

The shirt is way too large for me—Bradley's a foot shorter than me, and a foot wider at the shoulders. She's a muscular brick, I'm a signpost. Worse, I'm handcuffed. I consider tying the shirt around my waist, but wind up tying it under my armpits to maximize my body heat. Not easy with handcuffed hands, but nobody's around to see my undignified squirming. I always feel like my butt is huge, but Bradley's voluminous shirt tells me I'm twenty kinds of wrong. It doesn't quite reach my buttocks, let alone the front, but I feel infinitely better with some sort of cover.

Right. That's dignity taken care of.

Now let's blow this taco stand.

41

My first problem in escaping a subterranean prison in one of the deadliest parts of the world is getting the manacles off my feet. I've already rubbed my ankles raw. Blood mingles with the rust. Rob's right, the last thing I need is sepsis.

But sepsis will kill me tomorrow. Staying here might kill me today. In my beautiful new oversized, muddy, secondhand T-shirt, I plop my bare butt on a patch of smooth cold dirt right at the back of the room.

They say you have to warm up before you stretch. That's right. I feel so stiff, it's like rigor mortis has already kicked in. But losing half of my flexibility leaves me about three times as limber as most people. I seize my foot and drag it up for close inspection.

The manacles themselves are steel bands, perhaps an inch wide. Each has a large keyhole, rather like a handcuff lock. Sloppy welds attach each manacle to a yard of grimy greasy steel chain. These things have been here as long as the light fixtures.

Plus, my chilly, callused feet stink.

I finger each link in the chain, scrutinizing every bit of surface, even slipping a pinky into each link to check for flaws. The rusty links are just beginning to corrode, but still fundamentally solid—

No.

One of the links, right in the middle of the chain, has a notch. It's not natural wear. I fumble at the link, digging my thumbnail into the notch, scraping out loose rust and greasy gunk to expose its secret. A trick link? A weak spot?

It is a weak spot, sort of. Someone ground maybe a quarter of the way through the link. It's clearly deliberate, but I can't imagine why.

Then I understand.

Another prisoner wore these chains before me. Maybe last year, maybe decades ago. I can see the shadowy figure now, crouched in a cell just like this one. She's got her feet as close to the ring in the wall as she can manage, and pulled a desperate few inches of slack over to an outcropping of stone.

So she can scrape at the link. Wear it away. Grinding her hands into bloody pate.

She never finished.

If I grind at the chain, wearing away that same link, maybe whoever wears these chains after me can finish the job and get out.

Or the one after them.

That is *not* going to happen.

So, attack the locks.

"Bradley," I say.

"Yeah?"

"Do you have anything long and thin? A pen? A needle?"

Bradley gives this little laugh. "No. Neither does Rob."

I say, "I could pick the lock in a second with the metal clip off a ballpoint pen. A *plastic* clip."

"Heck, even *I* could do that given a whole second."

"Half a second per lock."

"Better. But no, we don't have anything to pick a lock with. They searched us pretty well."

I grimace, then turn my attention to the cave. "I knew a guy once," I say, "who carried lock picks with him on every gig."

"I do. They found them."

"No, Eric had them in this little plastic pouch." I methodically examine every inch of the cave wall. There must be something useful here. "Tied a string around his back molar and around the pouch, then swallowed it. Swore he'd never be kept."

"That's not a bad idea," Bradley says. "Did he happen to come with us?"

"Nope." Nobody's scratched anything helpful on the wall or left anything behind. All the little bulging protuberances conceal only more rock. "He got punched in the stomach. The tools punctured the pouch, he bled out before we could evac."

"Why Beaks, that's lovely. How up*lifting*."

"Point is, there might be something in these cells. Something they missed before putting us in." There's no notches in the walls, no secret shelves in the shadows. "Something that someone smuggled in, and left behind." No cubbyholes up in the darkened ceiling.

That leaves the floor.

I sink to my knees and jab my bare fingers at the floor.

The dirt has been hard-packed by who knows how many feet, jammed into the stone just like their hopes. I barely scrape the surface. When I finally get a chunk of dirt to shift, it's usually just a little divot packed into a dip in the stone. My fingers quickly grow tired and achy. I quickly fill my nails with dirt, then break the nails as I dig more. My breath deepens, but I try to only inhale on my left side to minimize the stab of the busted rib. Working warms me, but I can't afford to lose the sweat breaking out along my spine.

I can't afford to stay here, either.

I claw deeper into musty earth.

After maybe an hour and a half of bare-handed digging and scraping, I find… a tooth. It's a yellow incisor, the root stained brown. I silhouette it against the hallway light for study, feeling this irrational surge of triumph. Finding someone else's decrepit incisor buried beneath the floor of your cell is *not* a good sign.

But the tooth has a long, tapering root.

My heart starts hammering harder. The sudden shake of my fingers means I almost drop the tooth, but I clutch it close in my aching bloody fingers. My knees thank me as I twist from my crouch to sit and pull my ankle into my lap.

My foot is in my shadow. That's okay. I don't really need light for this.

The incisor's root is just barely small enough to fit into the lock around my ankle. It can't turn quite enough to get at the lock mechanism, though. That's okay. I don't force it. People have made tools out of tooth and bone for the last million years.

Why, with the manacle I even have a steel corner to grind the tooth against. What more could I ask for?

I make haste, but *slowly*. If I ruin this tooth, I'll have to knock out one of my own to get a replacement. If the work takes too long, I'll still be carving my key when Noah's thugs come to shoot me.

Picking a lock like that on the manacles takes an L-shaped tool. A tooth isn't even nearly the right shape, but I carefully grind away a notch into the tooth's side. If I can just get the tooth's grinding surface in the lock and turn it so that I can twiddle the mechanism, I can escape. Get Bradley and Rob out. Blow the hell out of this place.

Every few scrapes, I make myself stop to lift the tooth to the light and scrutinize my work. Better to stop too early, than to go too far.

I've got my tongue pushed hard into my own cheek, a soothing ache against my busted cheekbone, and my butt is freezing on the bare dirt. My own sweat glues the oversized dirty T-shirt to me, and I have to keep stopping to shake the tension out of my hands and shoulders. I haven't done any carving like this since Girl Scouts. It demands patience, and I don't *want* to be patient.

The light never changes. Insects don't herald dusk, and birds don't announce the dawn. I find a nice sharp burr on the edge of the manacle by scraping it across my thumb. Spatters of fresh blood mingle with powdered tooth.

It gets to the point where I can get the tooth into the hole and turn it a little. The notch isn't quite deep enough for the ninety degree swivel I need, so I ease it back out. A few more scrapes, and try again.

Almost.

My hands start shaking. I could really use an actual drink of water. I can probably suck a little more off the walls—but I can't wait. Pick this lock, and I'll go raid Bradley's bucket. Her beautiful, luxurious bucket of water. Fresh, cool—

No. I put the tooth down to massage my hands and relax my shoulders, deliberately inhaling deeply through my nose and exhaling between my lips.

The notch goes maybe two-thirds of the way into the tooth, exposing the black heart of the root. One more tiny scrape, almost walking the bone past the metal.

A delicate shaving of old enamel floats away.

Relax, Billie, I tell myself. You've done this blindfolded. Upside down. Under water. Locked inside a car trunk, on the conveyor belt to the crusher. This is a doddle.

The tooth goes into the manacle. It turns, easily.

I close my eyes. Looking won't help. This is all feel.

The tooth isn't a tool. It's an extension of my finger.

Feel through it.

Don't jab: *caress.*

Like you're stroking a baby's hair with one extra-long finger.

Below the notch, inside the lock, I ease the tooth up against the lock mechanism. A twist, a bump, and the manacle will open.

The lock is stiff, though. Probably full of dirt. Not used very often.

Hardly daring to breathe, I turn the tooth with my thumb and forefinger on the axle of its root. One degree at a time. Don't push it. Just a little further—

—*crack*—

The tooth gives this almost imperceptible shudder.

Inside the manacle, something rattles.

Falls free.

I'm quivering as I retract the tooth.

Snapped. Right at the carved notch.

I don't scream. Or cry. I don't do anything except study the tooth for a breath before I put it on this tiny outcropping of stone. Deke would be proud of me—

No.

To *hell* with Deke. He's why I'm here. If he gave any damn about me at all, even if Noah had turned him, he'd be down here to break me out. My mixed feelings separate like oil and water, and there's a whole lot more rage than love.

When I find Deke, I'm putting a bullet through his head.

I've dug up almost all the dirt floor within reach when I hear distant footsteps, echoing down the tunnel as they approach.

42

The good news is, my bruised and aching hands have acquired a protective crust of blood and mud. My knees and shins have fresh bruises from kneeling on increasingly exposed irregular rock. I'm parched, panting for air, and warmed only by my own efforts. The constant illumination of the dangling bulb in the tunnel feels like it's burned its way into my skull, adding to the pounding heat in my temples. My gown-sized T-shirt is stuck on me like muddy paper mache—you could cut it in half, slide me out of it, and use it to cast a torso just like from ancient Rome.

The bad news is, I've moved enough so that my raw ankles haven't scabbed. There's a slow but constant trickle of turgid gummy blood from beneath the heavy iron manacles. Small heaps of ancient dirt and tiny pits, some no wider than my pinky, cover the floor of my tiny alcove, so there's really no place to stand.

And I really hate being dirty. I'm not just dirty now—I'm plastered in earth, everywhere. I'm one of the Mud People. I don't want to even *think* about some of the places I've got dirt. I'm going to need a trip through the car wash just to get clean enough to take a shower before my bath.

The footsteps get closer. Who is it? The jailer?

Or, maybe, Noah himself?

Air hisses out between my clenched teeth as I climb to my feet. My calves tingle with returning blood, making me shift my weight back and forth to work out the needles. Sitting would be a nice break, but I'm not letting anyone see me on my knees. Not here.

The footsteps stop. A high, grating voice says, "Mister Robert Fender. What a pleasure to meet you at last."

"Jack Noah." Rob's voice sounds weak. Is he playing? Or is he hurt more badly than Bradley said? "Welcome to the party. I do hope you brought a bottle of palatable wine."

That *is* him. Sir Jack Noah. The man who hired Deke to infiltrate and ravage a company so he could claim control of it. The man who murdered our friends. The man who turned Deke.

It's all I can do to not scream. My jaw is clamped to my skull, my aching burning hands knotted into clubs.

Noah has this nasal *hee-hee* laugh. "The best, of course. We've had our dinner, but it'll do nicely as a nightcap." His voice loses any shred of charm. "We agreed that we would never meet. And yet you assaulted—no, *destroyed*, my home, and then you flew to the other side of the world to try to break in here. What were you trying to do?"

"Merely a job," Rob says.

"For who?" Noah says. "Who was dumb enough to hire the three of you to come after me? On foot? You're insane to attempt here with anything less than a helicopter gunship."

"Cost cutting gets to everyone eventually," Rob says.

"Oh really." Noah doesn't seem too interested in finding out who hired us. "You're an older gentleman. How would you like an additional lifetime?"

"That absurd body transplant project?" Rob says. "It'll never work."

"Neither will internal combustion," Noah says. "Heavier-than-air flight. Manned spaceflight. But here we are."

"For someone who's supposed to be so smart, you seem horribly attached to discredited ideas." Noah brushes imaginary lint off his shoulder. "But I'm not here to argue with you."

"No, you're here to gloat," I say.

"Now, why would I bother with that?" Noah spreads his hands to either side of his blooming belly. "I am here to express my sincere thanks. Without you, I wouldn't have the infamous Rob Fender here. I wouldn't have the opportunity to sway him to my cause."

"He won't help you either," I say.

"Everyone helps me," Noah says. "You helped me by releasing Butterfly Star Research's sickle cell data into the public. You'll even help me advance science tomorrow, once you get into the lab. Rob helped me by keeping me up to date on every move your little team made. Even your precious Donald Eckhart helped me, by telling me to clear the village and ambush you."

My thoughts dissolve into a torrent of red rage.

I throw myself forward, hands scratching for his face, heart jackhammering in my throat, not thinking of anything but ripping Noah's flabby meat right off his bones.

The rusty manacles catch my abused ankles before I've gone inches, yanking my feet out from under me, sending me sprawling onto the irregular rock of the cell floor, screaming in inchoate fury. My elbow hits a spur of rock, shooting pain up through my arm, but I'm outstretched and shrieking and clawing at Noah's ankles, not even six inches from the edge of my reach, iron gouging my feet, taste of dirt on my tongue, voice hoarse.

Noah says something. All I can hear is that it's calm, infuriatingly mocking.

Then he and his thug walk away, leaving me shrieking like an angel rising straight out of Hell.

43

The supernova of anger has hollowed me out. It's like my soul had a cyst that's finally ruptured, gushing my hurt over Deke's betrayal all over this ugly little subterranean cell, to mix with the dirt and rock and make the place even more toxic. I feel like I can start to heal. The wound in my psyche still hurts, it's just not pressing on me so fiercely.

Don't get me wrong—I'm still going to shoot Deke. But lying on the ground, covered in dirt, tears dripping into the rocky floor, my mind feels more clear than it has since Deke died. Faked his death. Betrayed me. Whatever.

My breath is starting to slow back to normal and the cave's clamminess sinking back into my skin when Bradley whispers, "Beaks?"

"Yeah, dammit." I don't bother whispering.

"He was *totally* gloating."

"No shit."

I drag myself back to my knees, then roll upright and plant my butt on this misshapen lumpy outcropping that's the closest thing I have to a flat surface in here. It feels like the cave's chill has seeped into my freshly hollowed heart.

I don't even have a tooth to carve into a key.

Surprisingly soon, more footsteps lumber down the tunnel. I wipe my face and struggle back to my feet. Thirst scorches my throat and makes my temples feel only loosely attached to my skull. My feet ache on the cold rock knobs of the misshapen floor. I have to hold the wall for balance, but I'm upright and defiant when that annoying naked bulb in the tunnel silhouettes my next visitor.

It's a woman. She can't be five feet tall, but her elaborately lacquered and pinned coiffure gives her another foot. She's all in white, from the pleated skirt that almost brushes the ground to her blouse. I've never thought Asians were expressionless, but she's showing more raw passion than I've seen in a long time—at least, anywhere but in a mirror. Her chin shakes. Unshed tears brighten her eyes. She's holding a pile of white and dark green cloth in her arms.

Beside and behind her looms another overmuscled thug in camouflage. He doesn't have a dart gun. Instead, he clenches a truncheon in one ham-hock fist.

A one-gallon steel pail dangles from his other hand.

A tow chain and a Mack truck couldn't yank my eyes from the pail. It weaves slightly with the weight of the water. The guard shifts his stance. A little surge splashes over the edge of the pail and crashes to the ground, scattering precious droplets into the dirt. Most rolls towards the meandering gutter, turning the thin trickle of water into a sudden short surge.

"You want?" the woman says.

Her voice does what that Mack truck couldn't. It has this veneer of comic-book politeness, but when I look away she's showing her teeth. Her eyes hold feral rage, mirroring me only a short time ago.

She holds up the pile of cloth. "Your clothes?"

Now that she says it, I recognize the outfit I'd worn in the Jeep. It's a shirt in my size, baggy camouflage pants. A corner of my bra peeks out from between the two. There might even be underwear in there.

"You want?" she says.

There's a trap here. I don't understand what's happening.

Not trusting my voice, I nod.

She gets a big phony smile and raises her hands over her head. "Oopsie!" The clothes topple to the dirt in my doorway, scattering shirt and underwear and everything through the dirt heaped around my cell.

I don't move. She wants me to crawl forward. To grovel in her feet to pick them up. I try to relax instead, keeping my knees and shoulders loose. I don't have much slack in this chain, but if this woman comes any closer I can probably punch her.

Instead, she takes the bucket from the thug. She doesn't bother taunting me. Instead, she hoists the bucket in both hands. Water gushes down into the torn-up dirt of my cell, soaking the clothes, splashing back out into the hall and down the tunnel into the infinite earth.

"Oopsie more!" she says.

I want to look down at the water, at the soaked clothes. Try to scoop something to drink out of the countless tiny stone fonts. The need to drink screams in the back of my head. Instead, I keep watch on the woman's crazed expression.

"Hold," she says. "I fix. I get you drink."

She takes a step back.

Sets the bucket on the ground.

Sweeps her long white skirt over it.

And squats.

I hear liquid trickle against the metal pail.

She stands. Lifts the pail. "For you!" The smile is huge.

I keep my face expressionless.

Her mockery shatters. Eyes narrow. Shoulders quiver, and the bucket shakes in her grip. "You kill my husband. He make you sleep—you, you kill him."

She swings the bucket up. About half of the contents coat the wall beside me. As for the other half, well… at least it's warm. For a moment.

My mind churns. I shot one of the tranquilizer-gun snipers. Killed him.

I know what this woman's feeling—I mean, I know *exactly* what she's feeling. And I know how far I'd go in her place.

I should have guessed. White. The color of mourning through lots of Asia.

I might be chained up in a cave, the grungiest I've ever been with all this dirt and sweat. An even filthier plutocrat plans to use me as an experimental animal.

But the most horrific threat I face is this bereaved woman.

Silhouetted by the stabbing light, Pissed Off Widow stares at me, nostrils flaring as her chest heaves, ready to charge me like an angry bull. The empty bucket dangles from two fingers, reflecting light against the cave walls.

She wants me to shout back at her. Her husband had "made me sleep," and I'd killed him with one of my last bullets. I feel this little surge of satisfaction, but quash it. I really didn't want to kill him—no. I take that back. Right then, when I'd been the last one standing, with a thiopental dart in my chest and Rob and Bradley prone around me, I'd wanted every one of them dead.

But what I wanted didn't matter.

I'd murdered her husband. Self-defense, but who cares?

And she wants me to pay.

I'm almost helpless, chained to the wall.

Doing nothing isn't a strategy.

But waiting for her to screw up is.

She stares up at my impassive face, her own face shadowed from the one light in the tunnel. Pissed Off Widow maybe comes up to my ribs, but right now she looks livid enough to chew her way through my sternum to my beating heart. Her pristine white mourning dress seems weirdly out of place down in these dank tunnels, and her towering hair, with all its pins and spray, woven with little gold beads, casts incongruous glittering reflections across the grim walls.

She steps towards me.

The thug next to her speaks urgently in some language I don't even recognize, and puts a massive hand on her tiny shoulder. She tries to shrug him off, then snaps back in the same tonal language when his hand doesn't even twitch.

I'm too dehydrated to sweat. My lips burn. Dirt is starting to flake off my skin, sending itches over every inch of my skin. The too-large T-shirt I'm wearing is so dirty, so glued to me, it's hard to tell where the cotton ends and my bare skin begins. The iron manacles set my abraded ankles aflame. I really want to sink to my knees and plunge my face into one of those shrinking puddles of water before the dirt entirely swallows them. Grab my sopping dirty pants from the muddy pit and suck every drop of moisture out of them. Instead, I keep my breathing steady and watch Pissed Off Widow's fuse burn shorter.

She relaxes.

The thug removes his hand.

"It means I die," she says. "But I see you scream."

And there's my plan—no, it's too simple, it doesn't deserve to be called a plan. But it's the best opportunity I've had since the chains went around my ankles.

"Your husband," I say. "When he died."

She glares at me. "You do not speak of him."

"He thanked me." I keep my voice flat and emotionless, even as I detest myself for what I'm about to say. "He hoped in his next life, he wouldn't be married to a pig."

Pissed Off Widow needs a moment to understand my English.

Then she's not merely pissed off.

She's incendiary.

Just like me a little while ago, she throws herself forward.

Unlike me, she has no manacles around her ankles to trip her up.

Her one hand catches my broken cheekbone. Pain slices through my skull and sparkling little lights fill my suddenly-monochrome vision. I sag against the wall and raise my handcuffed hands, catching one hand in that skyscraper hair, turning my right side towards the rock to protect my broken ribs.

She's punching my chest, my shoulder, without any skill but with a huge amount of strength. Even with my middling martial arts, I could sidestep those blows... if I wasn't chained to a wall, exhausted, dehydrated.

I shove at her again, as if I'm trying to get her off me.

Then she's yanked back. The thug is shouting at her in their singsong tongue—not Chinese, I know a little Mandarin and some Cantonese. I hold myself up against the wall, glad that I need the pretense of weakness. I look at the floor, as if I'm cowed, but inside my heart thrums in top gear.

Pissed Off Widow's white dress has all these stains now, from slamming against my unclean self. Her hair's still a skyscraper, but it's after the Big Quake and all crumpled and toppling. Her chest heaves, and her face has this flush that's one shade short of a heart attack. The thug's hands on her shoulders is the only reason I still have eyes or kidneys.

"I see you dead," she hisses. "I talk to lab, yes. Doctor always looks at me, I give him what he wants. No pain pills for you. You die screaming, and I laugh."

The thug tugs her away.

"You die! Die! I laugh! Bring your heart to my husband!"

I keep staring at the floor, trying to control my breathing and slow my heart. The dirt has absorbed the water, at best turning into a slurry. I pant limply until the widow's enraged screams echo into silence.

Once I'm absolutely certain she's gone and I'm alone, I open my hand.

Revealing a pair of plain, unadorned, absolutely gorgeous two-inch steel hair pins.

My shoulders quiver with excitement, the tension of a long-held arrow finally released but not yet flown, but my hands are steady as I bend Pissed Off Widow's first hairpin in the light from the tunnel.

I'd bragged that I'd need one second to open both manacles. The manacle around my left ankle takes a whole three seconds. I blame fatigue and dehydration. The second fights me for five seconds, but it seems there's a chunk of tooth wedged into the mechanism and the guards might be back any second. Freeing that foot will take too long.

Instead, I attack the cheap padlock attaching the manacles to the chain anchored in the wall. It gives in a handful of seconds. The handcuffs surrender in about the time it takes a Wall Street trader to trash a pension fund. I grab the free manacle in my right hand, ignore the manacle around that ankle, and tromp through the squishy mud into the tunnel.

The abrasions around my ankles and on top of my feet sting like mad, and my half-wet T-shirt clings to me like chilly mud. In the stark light everything seems more real, the smell of cold wet stone more cloying in my nose, my shadows razor-sharp with sudden adrenaline.

God, I want something to drink.

Or even that foil packet of brownies, abandoned on the irregular stone floor.

Instead, I trudge up the inclined tunnel to the next alcove.

Bradley's hole is a little bigger than mine, but more exposed to the tunnel. She's even got a little shelf of rock to sit on, with her legs stretched out to accommodate her own chains and wall ring. She's in khaki pants, an industrial bra, and dirty socks. Without a shirt, her bulky frame looks even tougher: tight muscles relaxed only by force of will, brown and red scars across light brown skin. Any fat she has must be hiding somewhere else.

Next to the hairpins, she's the second most beautiful thing I've ever seen.

No, *third*. Next to Bradley, on the outcropping, there's this translucent plastic gallon jug of clear, luscious water. Glimpsing it sets my thirst screaming.

Bradley's daydreaming eyes come fully alert when I stagger into view. Her jaw drops open, but she doesn't say a word.

Every part of me aches for the water. Instead, I sink to my knees at Bradley's feet and attack her manacles. Eagerness slows me, but it's still only one breath to get the first manacle and another for the second.

Bradley pulls her freed feet closer to her and leans to my ear to whisper, "Let me get Rob. You get a drink."

I hand her the hairpins like the precious treasures they are. She hands me the condensation-slick jug.

My mouth explodes in pain at the first mouthful, the taste of loose blood and garlic and who knows what. The second soothes. The third makes it all the way to my stomach in a cool pool of life, seeping into my veins. I make myself stop and breathe—we can't afford for me to puke this up.

At the next slug of water, sweat bursts from my entire body. I'm covered in dirt and worse, but it quickly softens to mud. I waste a handful sluicing the worst of the filth off my face, clearing my eyes and lips, then it's another slow draught.

Rob and Bradley return before I swallow. Rob somehow makes the drab khaki pants, white T-shirt, and socks elegant and crisp, but the expression on his face says he's ready to fight hippos barehanded. He gives me a quick, broad smile and leans in to whisper "Darling Beaks."

His words lift my spirits.

But his offered foil packet of protein bar—no, *two* bars!— hoists them into orbit. I tremble with eagerness, but force myself to chew thoroughly between bites. My body tingles everywhere as the water and food resurrect me.

Bradley disappears, but returns with the packet of brownie. She leans closer as I tear the seal. "Damn, woman. How did you manage to get my shirt that dirty?"

"I'm good," I say before stuffing my face.

Bradley kneels to pick my remaining manacle. "What the hell did you do to this?"

I swallow. "Carved a pick out of a tooth. It broke."

Bradley's hands freeze. She looks up with awed respect, staring at my mouth.

"Not my tooth," I say. "Someone left it."

Bradley raises her chin in acknowledgement, then turns back to her work. It takes her almost a minute, but the manacle groans open.

I'm free.

Rob rescues my soiled, damp clothes, and tries to quietly shake the worst of the dirt out of them. They're wet, but I don't care—they're mine. My borrowed shirt is so wet it doesn't leave me any modesty, so I peel right out of it and pull on the clammy cotton underwear we'd traveled in.

Once I get out of here, I'm getting in a hot shower and not getting out for a week.

Maybe two.

Bradley's stretching as I get dressed, crudely limbering up her shoulders and hips. Rob watches up the tunnel—mostly because someone needs to watch, but also with a shred of gentlemanliness.

Dirty as I am, dirty as the clothes are, getting my butt properly covered again feels great.

I slip my arms into the bra and reach around to clip it. My broken rib stabs my side and I hiss involuntarily.

"Problem?" Bradley whispers.

"Broken rib," I hiss. It seems to be a lower rib, I can probably clip it in front, turn it around, and weasel into it. If it was an upper rib, I wouldn't have a chance.

"Turn around," Bradley says.

I turn. "Second hook."

At least I don't have to get a balaclava over my broken cheekbone. The swelling probably even provides some black-and-blue camouflage.

I hold up my last piece of clothing, a T-shirt with sweat-stained armpits. "Bradley, can I pay you back?"

She doesn't even glance at me. "Pecan brownies or nothing, bitch."

I don't take offense—Bradley's psyching herself up. With good reason. "You're on." Pulling the shirt over my head I say, "Thought you might like not showing off the goods."

Bradley shows teeth. It's not a smile. "Asshole looks at my cleavage? Gives me time to break his neck."

I study the muddy socks for a second. My ankles are rubbed raw—leaving them exposed is better than rubbing filth right into them. The socks get stuffed into a back pocket. Maybe I can use them as a gag. I lift my manacles, still connected together by three feet of chain, and sling them over one shoulder. I don't know what I'll need them for, but these lengths of greasy rusty metal are the only tools we have.

"Ready," I whisper.

Rob's still looking up the tunnel, but he turns so Bradley and I can hear his quiet voice. "Bradley. Do you want to direct?"

"Huh?" Bradley says.

"Noah claimed that I kept him up to date on our progress."

"If you did," I say, "you didn't know about it. Just because we didn't find your comm codes in his email, doesn't mean Deke didn't tell him."

"That's right," Bradley says. "Don't go wimping out on us now."

Rob gives this thin, worried smile and dips his chin. "I'm never one to refuse a lady's wishes." His eyes get hard again. "We're in no shape to fight anything out. The goal is escape. We target Noah, and Deke, another time."

Our best hope is that Noah told us the truth. That it's after dinner. If we're lucky, the guards have locked us in for the night. And hopefully they leave the lights on all night. The thought of trying this stunt in subterranean darkness terrifies me.

And if the lights go off half-way through? I'm dead.

But I still kind of hope that the guards come down to check on us. Bring us a bedtime mint, turn down our blankets, offer a peck on the cheek. Because my plan's only slightly less foolhardy than waiting to be used as an experimental animal. At least in the lab, I'd probably live longer.

My legs have tightened up—I can't even get all the way into the splits. Maybe if I'd warmed up first with a few kata, but we don't have that kind of time. The actual depth of the stretch isn't as important as loosening up the muscles, though. I hold my weight on my hands and slowly empty and refill my lungs, trying to drain the torrent of fear and worry and anger and general distress out of my brain. My broken rib stabs at each breath, but I try to ease myself around it. Accept the pain, rather than fight it.

It works, so long as I breathe slowly.

This stunt demands absolute, unwavering concentration. Kind of like a Zen master, but with focus.

We don't have a clock, so I hold each pose for twenty slow breaths—long enough to get the blood flowing through every part of my body. When I turn and ease my weight off my hands, I twist my arms and shoulders back and forth as I'm stretching my legs, trying to work the sand out of my joints.

I go through five poses, twenty breaths on each, before I feel loose enough to even attempt this. Any more stretching won't improve my odds of success, only put off the beginning. I roll to my feet, feeling more relaxed than I have since deciding to avoid flying Emirates Air and the accompanying death warrants.

Rob leans close to whisper, "I have complete faith in you."

"Glad one of us does," I whisper back, softening it with a smile.

Bradley gives me a stern, comradely nod. "I'll be waiting for the fun to start." She leads us back up to just short of the final turn, where the cameras can almost but not quite see us.

The lights are mounted ten feet up. Above them, the wall rises into darkness. I'm hoping the ceiling is another dozen yards past them.

The left wall looks a little less steep than the right, and it's on the inside of the curve. Sadly, by what Bradley described, I need the right wall.

My plan sounded simple enough. Start around the curve, where the cameras can't see. Climb the wall. Get high enough that I'm above the camera's field of vision, hidden in the darkness that swallows the ceiling. Crawl around the wall and down above the cameras. Look at the door, the cameras, and figure out the next step.

Just like a video game.

But this isn't a video game, and I don't have any extra lives.

I back a few more feet down the tunnel for the extra distance from the cameras, pick a spot, and start to climb.

The first few feet are straightforward. My heartbeat picks up, but not enough to distract me. The unfinished, rough walls offer countless little ledges and protrusions where my feet can get a good grip. I move patiently, making sure I have three of my limbs firmly placed before I move the fourth.

These walls are warmer than the ones in the cells further down, and drier. We must be really close to the surface here. For a moment I wonder if it might be night, and the darkness overhead actually a cloud-choked sky—but no, there's no breeze. I can't see much past the lights, only enough to know it's there. No smells but dust and stone and the faint hint of distant dampness.

Climbing goes pretty easily until I get above the lights.

The light fixtures cast lines of shade upwards into the cave's gallery. More rocky extrusions cast their own shadows, slicing the upper part of the cave into a deformed kaleidoscope of light and shade across rocks of brown and green and gray. A spur of darkness might be a safe place to put my foot, or merely the shadow of an outcropping far below. Sweat trickles down my spine, and I have to stop more than once to slow my breath. I test each grip for solidity before relying on it, careful to not put weight on my ribs.

I have to climb pretty high to get above the camera's field of vision. How big is that field? I won't know until I blaze a path around the curve and can see the cameras themselves.

So I climb as high as I dare. The higher I go, the more the shadows cloak the stone, the further apart the handholds get, and the steeper the wall rises.

About thirty feet off the ground, I stop. The wall isn't quite vertical. Not *quite*. The grips are almost far enough apart that I don't dare climb any further. The ceiling gleams dimly from reflected light, maybe twenty feet further up, so the walls have got to start turning inward within the next few feet even if I can't make out exactly where that happens.

So I start scooting sideways, one handhold at a time, trying not to sweat.

Crossing ten horizontal feet takes about forever. I've been able to keep my weight on my feet the whole time, avoiding those exhausting two-hand dangles that suck your strength out of you like water from a punctured balloon. With my hurt rib, taking my weight on an arm means falling. But at that point, I can see a sliver of brick wall at the far end.

Now, as I make each lurching exchange of anchors, hugging the wall for the minuscule support the vague slope offers, I need to watch out for the first camera. If it's aimed too high I need to retreat, slither a few feet further up the wall, and try again.

The floor gapes beneath me, sucking at my soul.

I should have let Rob try the sick prisoner gag.

Eventually, I get far enough around the curve to see the wall blocking our escape.

The brick wall isn't cinderblock. It's actual solid bricks, mortared firmly together. This is a sledgehammer-resistant wall. Even at this distance, I can make out a few chips and knocks from old blows. Bullet scars, maybe?

A metal rail, painted white but spotted with rust and grime, runs along the wall, right on the ground. Another rail crosses the wall about ten feet up. Tracks, for the big sliding door Bradley described.

I reach out with my left foot, toes questing for a place to stand in a likely shadow. There's a ledge in the darkness, a nice solid one, maybe six inches wide but higher than I'd like. I can have both feet on something solid simultaneously, but I'd be dangerously close to doing the splits. I'll never hold my balance that way. I have two solid grips.

It's time to swing both feet free. It's a stupid risk in a normal free climb, but this whole thing is a stupid risk.

I relax a moment, easing my grips just a little. Fingers tingle. Flex one hand, then the other. Grab tight, then guide the left foot forward.

Jump off the right.

For a horrifying second both feet swing free across the stone, sending a rain of dust down the wall to the floor. My damaged ribs shriek their outrage, almost making me pull my right hand free. My left foot finds the ledge easily, and I dig the toes in like I'm at the beach and immediately freeze.

I should relax.

But I can see the first camera now.

I make myself hold still while I study it. If it's a really expensive full-spectrum camera, one that can do infrared and visible light simultaneously, and if it's aimed high enough, I already stand out like a fire in the night. If they've already noticed me, I'm screwed. But if it's a regular camera, if I hold still in this broken shadow, they probably won't notice me.

The camera's the size of a milk carton, mounted right above the upper door track.

It's angled down, for a better view of the tunnel floor as it drops away.

Best of all, I can't tell what type it is.

Because there's an aluminum hood, to protect it from the glare of the lights.

I'm high enough up. Even my feet are high enough up.

They can't see me.

I want to call down in triumph, to let Rob and Bradley know that we're okay. I turn my head to see them, a few yards behind and disturbingly far below. Bradley's standing relaxed, bent at the waist to touch her toes. Rob's looking up into the darkness where I disappeared. His gaze tracks forward, to my perch and beyond.

He can't see me.

Any sound I make will carry to the cameras, and the presumptive microphones, just as well as it will reach him.

Stick to the plan.

I climb forward, supported by carefully selected foot rests and hope.

48

As the cavern gallery walls grow further apart, the bulbs on the far side reflect a little more illumination up onto my human fly impression. Each handhold and toehold seems further and further apart, piling more strain on that busted rib. I struggle between eagerness and fear the whole way, constantly reminding myself that if I slip I'll plunge thirty feet to the dirt and stone floor.

And any medical team that shows up won't be to rescue me.

Noah orders guards executed for abusing prisoners. He probably orders the same for guards who don't notice someone falling into camera view. They'll be alert.

I'm exhausted. The lower ribs on my right side hurt, though I nurse them at every grab. My back aches with the strain of the climb. My feet are bruised from probing for footholds.

Another fifty slippery, treacherous feet until I reach the brick wall.

This was a terrible idea.

Maybe the only idea. But a terrible one nonetheless.

I'm *so* ready for this climb to end.

But the only way this ends is when I finish.

Or I plummet to my (increasingly likely) death.

So I fumble, and stretch for holds, and struggle to control my breathing and try to keep my clammy sweat from blinding me.

Or making my grip even more slippery.

Another five feet, though, and my questing knee discovers a stabby-sharp corner in the wall.

It's not stone, like the wall.

It's metal.

I have to peer through the shade for a couple minutes to figure out what I've found. It's a long, angular shape hugging the cavern wall stretching away towards the brick.

And then I laugh with relief.

In a previous age, someone mounted lights way up here. The lights aren't in use any more. I'm guessing that the elderly wiring died, and Noah had less expensive lights mounted at a lower level.

But the mounting rail is still up here, anchored to the wall.

I cross the next forty feet with my feet on a rusty, grungy, but fairly solid metal rail. The wall slopes outward just enough to ease the passage, giving me just a tiny bit of space to lean. Even testing the surface each time I take a step, I only need a few minutes to finally put my left hand on the brick wall at the front of the cave.

The brick feels just as solid thirty feet up as it looks at ground level: coarse, gritty, and ready to stand until the cockroaches and rats claim the world we're ruining. The bricks are roughly chopped to fit against the stone, the gaps fully plugged by mortar. Even up here the brickwork feels tight, barely wide enough for me to slip a fingertip in. My toes wouldn't possibly fit.

So close to the end, I have to force myself to move slowly. Normally I'd focus on my breath to calm myself, but every deep inhalation triggers a jolt of pain from my broken ribs. I hug against the steep cliff to catch my breath, but the touch of rock lights up my broken cheekbone. My muscles want to clench in excitement, but that leads straight to exhaustion.

And falling.

The good news is, the cameras above the big steel door don't cover the corners where brick wall meets cave wall. If I fall to my death from here, the guards won't see. Eventually, Rob and Bradley will peek around the corner and see my shattered corpse in the corner, feet pointing at the sky and head jammed into my lungs.

But they're not going to see that. Because I'm going to get down.

Handholds and footholds grow more numerous and closer together as I descend. In a surprisingly short time, I get to the reason I climbed this wall rather than the less steep wall.

The door tracks.

There's a huge metal door in the wall, maybe ten feet square, painted white but bubbled with breakthrough rust. It slides towards me, between metal tracks that come within about a foot of the cave wall. The upper track is about four, five inches wide at the top, and nicely flat.

I find a big, solid outcropping of rock to stand on, right in the corner where stone touches brick. It's a foot higher than I'd like, but it has enough space for me to squirm my left foot around.

Deep slow breath. Another. Accept the stab of broken rib. Is it getting worse? Doesn't matter right now—you're still breathing, it hasn't punctured a lung yet. Maybe it's just fractured, or bruised—no, it doesn't matter. Breathe.

Wipe my left hand on a dry patch on my khaki pants.

Seize a good, solid handhold on a knob of rock a few inches from the brick.

Squirm my left foot on its shelf so I'm standing pigeon-toed. The heel is pressed hard against the brick, my toes pointed somewhat back along the cave.

Relax the shoulders.

And swing my right hip and shoulder into open air.

Two points on. Two points way, way off.

I wobble, and breathe, and relax, as I swivel my body further over open air.

After a minor eternity, my shoulders touch brick.

My butt follows a beat after.

Some of my tension eases—but there's no time to relax.

Slide my right foot down the wall.

My left hand aches with the intensity of my grip. The stone feels dry. Dusty. Maybe even loose. My palm sweats. I bend my left knee, trying to ease the strain.

Right foot inches down. It should have touched the door track by now.

Have I somehow entirely missed the track? No, I couldn't have.

Sweat stings my eyes.

Beneath that right foot, empty space.

Just like everything in front of me.

My pulse threatens to shake me off the wall.

Then my toes touch cool hard steel.

Ease my foot down, until the heel rests on solid metal.

My right hand hugs the wall, clawing for feeble traction in the negligible gaps between the gray concrete bricks.

Empty my lungs. Relax my shoulder. Ease the death grip on the irregular cave wall. My stance is awkward, with my left leg bent almost double at the knee, but I must let go of the tension rippling through me. I can't wear myself out in a continuous clench, I'll need that strength soon.

I can't see my foot on the track. My own body's in the way. I tighten my grip on the cave wall and take the weight off that foot so I can use it to explore. Edging it back, I find twelve, maybe fourteen inches between my foot and the near end of the track. Plenty of space.

I plant the right foot firmly on the steel track, heel firm against the brick wall.

Release my death grip on the knob of rock.

Focus on my balance.

And slowly—*slowly*—ease the other foot onto the steel track.

Once I have both feet on the rail, skewed sideways so that I can get the balls of my feet on that narrow steel surface, I pause again to deliberately relax.

Then, one excruciating inch at a time, I shuffle down the track, away from the wall. Each step feels quick. Actually covering distance takes forever.

Finally, my leading toes touch the welded crosspiece of the closest camera mount.

I freeze. Shuffle a couple vital inches towards the friendly slope of the cave wall.

And even more slowly, crouch.

I keep my butt against the brick—but gently! I don't need *any* forward pressure. There's the constant urge to clutch the wall, to dig my fingers in, but that leads to pushing, and pushing leads to falling. I'm only ten feet above the ground, but the open space before me yawns like a vacuum, sucking at my bones. My breath is shallow and tight—if I breathe too deep the rib will stab me, I'll flinch, I'll unbalance, I'll fall.

More sweat runs into my eyes and soaks my armpits, but I don't dare wipe it away.

Instead, I close my eyes. Seeing won't help. Not now. I can't see what my hand quests for, my own shoulder's in the way.

My knees bend, stretching out to the side.

But eventually, my fingers touch the knobby steel rod of the camera bracket.

Careful! Don't joggle the camera. Don't give whoever's watching the camera a wibbly-wobbly announcement that something's wrong. What would they think, that a stray raccoon got up here? Maybe cave fish? Might as well be cave vultures. I can't bend to look, not without falling over, so I keep my eyes closed. My busted ribs jab with every breath now; I've got to get them taped up.

The camera mount is a steel rod welded perpendicular to the top of the track. I yearn to lean on it, to use its width for extra balance. That would move the camera, though. Instead, I spider my fingers forward until I gently brush the back of the rectangular camera itself.

The camera has one cable going into it. It's a networked camera, fed electricity by the same wire that carries the signal back through the wall. Eyes still closed,

I follow the cable back to where it slips into a rubber-edged pencil hole drilled through the brick wall.

Now to unplug it.

The camera is housed in a plastic weatherproof shell, with an aluminum awning over it to shade the lens. My fingers gently stroke the slick plastic belly. There—a hair-thin line in the plastic, just in front of where the cable enters the camera.

A sliding cover.

Hardly daring breathe, I painstakingly coax the cover off the camera. Every motion threatens to steal my balance. My calves are burning from doing the squats, but I can't stand back up. Not when I'm so close. In a moment, though, the plastic cover slides free of the camera.

While it would be easy to drop the cover to the ground, and there's no way anyone could see it, I pull it back in my hand to grip it between my pinky and palm. I can always drop the cover, but once it's on the ground I can't retrieve it.

My thumb and forefinger trace the cable to its socket. After all this work, actually disconnecting the camera takes only pushing on a flimsy plastic tab and slipping the cable out of its socket.

The guard on the other side of this wall has just had a screen go black.

With any kind of luck, their procedure says to investigate.

Straightening my legs, my calves cry as fresh blood hits them again. To help hold my balance, I slide my right foot a critical few inches to the right so that it rests on the protruding camera bracket.

If the door remains shut for ten minutes, I'm to slide over and disconnect the other camera and blind the guard station, then grab Rob and Bradley so we can break the door open somehow.

Maybe nobody's guarding the cave.

Or maybe Noah has another camera hidden in the rocky ceiling. Perhaps he's been eating popcorn for the last hour, chortling over my foolish and unnecessary free climb.

Or maybe the guard will pump the place full of VX nerve gas and melt our faces off.

There might not even be a guard. They might trust the manacles and the freaking huge steel door and its buried latch mechanism.

No, don't think that. Don't distract yourself. Stay right here. Breathe and balance.

In only a moment, a *thunk* ripples through the rail. The vibration hits my feet and echoes up my legs, making me wobble.

A *clank* and a *bonk* follow.

I grin with triumph.

But then the door rolls beneath me with a metallic screech, sending dozens of conflicting vibrations through the metal rail. The door smashes into the end of the track with an ear-splitting crash of metal against metal, setting me rocking.

Instinctively, I lean back against the wall.

But there's no room to lean.

My shoulders bounce off the brick, and I'm toppling towards the rocky floor below.

Right in front of whoever opened the door.

49

Falling ten feet takes about a sneeze.

Fortunately, Deke had me practice falling. First, backfalls onto a tatami mat. Then, a few feet off the ground onto a thick inflated bag. Then a few feet off the ground onto a tatami mat. Then we played "pretend this airplane is going down hard" and jumped with parachutes.

All of that's a far cry from a ten-foot drop onto the hard-packed dirt and rock of a cavern floor.

As I overbalance, when my stomach turns hollow and my inner ear shrieks its primal warning, I kick off the rail and transform the fall into a jump. I'd rather break an ankle than a neck.

A split-second of soaring freedom. I have almost enough time to close my teeth and tuck my chin to my chest.

My feet strike unyielding rock.

I let my knees and waist crumple with the impact, rolling sideways, arms slapping out to absorb some of the shock, letting the blow squeeze the air of me.

My busted ribs shriek as I roll over them. It takes everything to not scream as agony spotlights the whole right side of my chest.

Brown sand puffs up in front of my face.

I keep rolling, though.

Just like in practice I come up on one knee, facing the door.

The big steel sliding door is open. I can't make out any detail in the space beyond, but it's brightly lit and the air gushing in tastes of oil and ozone and growing greens.

This spindly kid, maybe eighteen or twenty, in jungle camo fatigues stands right inside the huge steel door to the cave-prison. His head is cocked to the side and his mouth dangles loose in shock. His head's buzzed close to the scalp, exposing an unfortunately lumpy skull guaranteed to chase off all the girls. He's dropped an aluminum stepladder.

Surprise won't hold him long. I have to put him down—fast.

I try to inhale.

The broken ribs scream.

The pain freezes me. It's not that the air is knocked out of me—my diaphragm aches to pull in a breath, but the ribs shifted when I fell, when I rolled.

Maybe I could have avoided that by rolling on the left side, but I always practiced rolling on the right.

If I get out of here, I'm practicing left side rolls.

But if I don't get to my feet right now, the whole climb, picking locks, soiling Pissed Off Widow's memory of her husband, all that's for nothing.

Head whirling, I thrust up on my feet and charge towards the kid.

The kid's hand fumbles at his waist.

His holster's empty—small favors.

The kid's shout carries his alarm, even in that unfamiliar tonal language, and he steps back.

My head's pounding with oxygen deprivation. My diaphragm expands through my chest pain, slowly hauling air in, but not nearly fast enough to make up for my hammering heart and what I'm burning by lumbering at the kid.

The kid raises his hands and takes a step back.

Someone beyond the door shouts.

Everything's losing its color, infusing with gray.

But I can still crash my left shoulder into the kid's scrawny chest.

He stumbles back, piling into this giant overmuscled thug—the guy who came down with Pissed Off Widow. He's got an expression now, and it's not a happy one.

I ricochet right off the kid.

Everything is gray now. Full of static. The gray ring around the edges of my vision is turning to black.

I've got to stop.

Stabilize those ribs.

Before I suffocate on my feet.

Breathe.

Instead, my arms hit the rough cavern wall.

Distant pain scrapes my forearms.

I roll to put my back to the wall.

Move, you lazy bitch. Move!

But my knees are getting weak.

The kid and the thug are untangled.

Both are looking at me.

The only thing holding me up is the wall.

At the far end of the tunnel of anoxia, the thug raises his truncheon.

50

If I don't move, I die.

Moving means breathing. Breathing means pain.

Maybe the lung is punctured.

If it is, I'm dead.

Fingers digging into the ragged cavern wall, I pull in a breath.

It's agony. Some bastard's dipped the right side of my chest in jellied gasoline and thrown a match.

The gray ring around my vision stabilizes.

I push the air out and drag in more.

My mouth is full of the bright coppery taste of fear—but not the sharper tang of blood. I'm not exhaling blood. Not yet.

I can see again, almost.

The kid stands a few feet from the huge square doorway, babbling into a little radio as he stares at me. He's twitching, feet shuffling in excitement, almost tripping over the forgotten aluminum stepladder he'd carried in.

The giant thug has his truncheon level with his head. He's walking towards me with this flat, affectless expression. He might be daydreaming about taking out the trash or reviewing his shopping list.

I need to stand up. Get my hands up. In front of me. Get ready to sidestep, to duck, to put the thug down.

But when I try to pull myself away from the wall, my knees wobble.

I slide another inch down the wall.

The thug takes another step closer.

I am *not* going down like this.

Except that I am.

I can breathe… so long as I don't move.

That's when Freight Train Liza Bradley runs the thug over.

The last time Bradley and I (and Deke) had worked together, she and Terry Watson got into a martial arts pissing contest before the gig started. They spent a good half hour exchanging these fancy locks and throws, stuff you'd have to practice for years to even try. I had to concede it was spectacular, but didn't want to say I figured it was completely useless in the real world.

All that fancy stuff?

She skips it.

Bradley's charging at full speed when she throws this vicious stomp kick right at the thug's knee. Bone splinters. I flinch in involuntary sympathy. Before the thug can even start to fall, she delivers a hammer fist into the back of his head. It's all techniques I know, but delivered with incredible force and stunning elegance.

The thug's eyes are on me. Then they're closed. I don't think he even knew what hit him.

Before the thug reaches the ground, Bradley's at the kid. A front kick to the groin, and there's another revolting crunch as his pelvis snaps. The heel of her hand goes into his nose. The kid's head snaps back.

He stops talking mid-word. Topples straight back.

The massive steel door abruptly starts sliding shut—someone's hit the panic button. They're going to seal us in. Come back with poison gas or machine guns. Even through the agony of breathing, I let out this thin keen of despair.

The door closes as quickly as it opened—

—except for Bradley.

She doesn't even slow as she scoops the kid's abandoned ladder and thrusts it sideways into the narrowing gap.

The steel door crunches the aluminum ladder with an ear-rending clang. The ladder crumples, bending into a shallow V, almost flat at the point of impact, but the door bounces open a yard or so and stalls.

Then Bradley's through the door.

At this angle, I can only glimpse a narrow slice of a desk and some open space past it. The screams come through just fine, though. So do the gunshots. And the extra screams. A couple faint snaps from more bones breaking.

Another gunshot.

Rob comes running up. He's huffing at his charge up the slope, obviously worn out, but his eyes are clear and his motions economical.

Another thug tumbles out of the room, staggering into our prison, fighting for balance on the rocky sandy ground even as he stares over his shoulder at Bradley. He looks horrified.

Rob veers.

The thug sees him coming, tries to get his hands up—but it's way, *way* too late.

Rob intercepts him. Matches his speed and motion. Wraps his arms around the thug's arms and neck, and pirouettes.

The thug whirls in a tight orbit around Rob. They're almost dancing.

Except for the part where Rob throws the thug's body to the ground—but keeps his head spinning the other way.

There's the gut-stabbing *snap* of a shattering spine.

Then Rob's through the doorway.

There's silence.

I focus on breathing through the pain.

Bradley trots back out through the half-open door. "Beaks! What's wrong?" She's barely breathing hard, and her face has this warm glow. The crazy lady *enjoyed* herself.

"Ribs," I wheeze. "Shifted."

She grimaces. Studies my mouth.

I open my jaw wide, heaving a breath out. It's not a cough, but it's the closest I can manage.

"No blood," she says.

I'm going to live. I'm not sure that's a good thing. Everything hurts.

"Back in second," Bradley says. She trots back through the door, returning with a small green canvas handbag in one hand and a fresh roll of dark green duct tape in the other.

Breathing is getting, well, not easier, but less horrible. Maybe I haven't destroyed my busted ribs—it might just be the shock of rolling over on them like an idiot.

"Can you get your arms up?" Bradley asks.

The ribs protest in flame, but I hoist my elbows chicken-style.

Bradley pulls my shirt up, not gently but without unnecessary force. "Give me the bad side."

"Duct tape," I say. "The miracle treatment."

"You know it. Does this hurt?"

I hiss through my clamped jaw.

"I'll take that as yes. How 'bout here."

My eyes watering, I manage, "Not so bad."

"Lower ribs. Bruised, a little fractured, not really busted. Not life-threatening, but painful as hell." Bradley rips off strips of tape, undoes my bra, and starts working under my right armpit. In a few days I'm going to itch like mad from duct tape glue, and I'll be happy to have the problem. Each jerk as she applies tape hurts, but the layers of tape drag the pain back to a manageable intensity. I can almost breathe normally.

Bradley clips my bra over the tape and rips open a pill packet. "Ibuprofen."

I pull my shirt down and dry-swallow the capsules. "Thanks."

"You good?"

I still ache everywhere, but breathing easily eases many pains. A drink would help more. Maybe a protein bar. No, not one of those dry things in a wrapper. A protein bar like a salad bar, with smoked salmon and grilled steak. Salad and chilled fruit on the side. In Tahiti. "Yeah."

"Good," Bradley says. "We've got a job for you."

51

The room beyond the prison caverns has very definite ideas of who belongs on the inside and who doesn't. It combines 1940s "keep the bombs out" construction techniques with modern military technology, in the name of defending really horrible human beings.

Maybe if those people weren't so awful, they wouldn't need these kinds of defenses.

The walls, all heavy gray brick, all look solid enough to resist anything up to a twelve-inch gun. No windows. Big flat screens on the walls, more screens on tiny wooden desks. Flimsy tranquilizer rifles on one wall rack, AK-74 assault rifles in another, with a whole bunch of the 30-round magazines and a few 45-round drums. A third rack with one empty peg holds a bunch of the old, bulky night vision goggles, the kind that gives you a headache after two minutes just from their weight. A broad area along one wall, set off with a low wall, corrals any prisoners as they pass from the heavy steel double doors in the front of the room and the cave entrance at the back.

And broken bodies, *everywhere*. A dozen men in cheap knock-off camo uniforms, all sprawled unconscious or dead. Knees and elbows and necks and thighs at impossible angles, and lots of busted noses oozing blood. One straight-back wooden chair, its wicker seat busted out, is jammed over the head and shoulders of a guard. The only way they're getting him out of there is with a saw, but he's not in a hurry. Never will hurry again.

Rob looks up as we come in. He's just finished checking a guard's pulse, shaking his head.

"Glad you could come to my party," I say. The duct tape pulls the right side of my torso, but it's infinitely better than the stab when I breathe. I'm gonna be rubbing glue out of my armpit for *weeks*.

"I fear it's—" Rob tears another strip of duct tape and starts on the man's ankles. "—rather tame so far." He looks tired, brown face sallow and eyes bloodshot.

"I don't know, Bradley seems to be having fun."

Bradley gives this big grin. "My fun's just starting."

"Security console," Rob says, pointing with his chin.

The big computer on the far wall isn't just for show. It's a common physical security management software setup. The first thing I do is grab the mouse and wiggle it, deferring the screen saver so we're not locked out.

The forty-inch screen above this console shows an idealized map of Noah's facility. A jagged blue line indicates the perimeter, intersecting squares for guard stations. Yellow squares and rectangles represent buildings, while green marks roads and footpaths.

Best of all, all the menus are in English. The guards might be more efficient in their native language, but like every greedy bastard I've ever robbed, Noah refuses to rely on translators for his physical security. He wants to understand what the security system's telling him, even if the guards work more slowly.

This room isn't the prison guardhouse.

It's the security nerve center for the whole compound.

The wicker-seated wooden chair feels plush when I sit. My legs immediately announce that they're done for the week, and I can't help groaning.

"Luxury later," Bradley says. "Out now."

The clock shows it's one AM, local time. Good. I start clicking through options, setting the screen flickering as fast as I can read.

Behind me Bradley says, "You're giving me a headache."

"Not my fault you can't keep up," I say. "Check the fridge, see what the caterer's done." And I sink into the computer, absorbing knowledge fast as I can. Redundant generators off to the side, near the reinforced gate and a narrow road that weaves towards China. No link out of here—no telecom, no data. Two boat docks, one large and one small, right down at the bottom of the hill. Datacenter, right inside the hospital. Quarters. Noah's home. Guest cottages—

Deke!

There's his name on a cottage. Right down by the water.

My hands pause for a second.

Deke's here. Everything in my gut knows it.

But we're totally blown.

And Rob's about done in.

I want Deke. But I'm not sacrificing Rob. Or Bradley, for that matter, but Bradley's tougher. She could do it with me. My ribs are taped up—they're not comfy, but I'd manage. We hold the escape for an hour, just to separate Noah's head from his flabby body. Find Deke. Get out. Miller Time.

My hand wavers over the mouse.

So close, it burns like an iron stake pounded through my heart.

But I steel myself and click to another view of the compound.

Then I hit the hospital, and stop again.

Twelve people.

Experimental chemotherapy drugs derived from an intriguing newly-discovered Amazonian beetle.

No, twelve *survivors*. They lost five with today's dose. *Noah, you—*

I stop myself again. I loathe that we're going to run. One day, I'm going to crush Noah. I'm coming back with a damn army and burning everything he loves to ash and greasy cinders, everything he's worked for, even if I have to steal the Mona Lisa and Michelangelo's David to pay for it.

I'm flipping through the electrical system information, absorbing everything, when Rob says, "What sort of set do we have?"

I jump a little. I hadn't noticed him come up behind me. I hadn't noticed someone setting the big glass of water by my hand, either. I give my head a little shake to clear the hacker's coma and grab the water. "We're in the nerve center for the whole place." The water tastes flat and tepid and delicious, even with chlorination. "We're uphill of most of it." I flip the big screen back to the large-scale map. "There, at the far left, that square? That's us. The big rectangle just next to it is the hospital, then there's the barracks, quarters."

"Defenses?"

"Electrified fence on three sides, river on the bottom. Access is by helicopter—the round circle, there. Or by boat. There's a little motor pool, right there, but the gate is narrow. The road's probably just as bad as what we took here. Docks down at the bottom. Eight guard towers, one at each corner and at each midpoint. And it's not just guards, either." I flip another screen up, bringing up a black-and-green night vision view. "Each tower has a remote-control turret with full-spectrum cameras. If someone shoots the poor bastards at the perimeter, the video gamers in here can just take over."

Rob studies the map.

"What's the extraction?" I say.

"Chopper," he says.

The water doesn't taste as good any more, but I force a little more down. A surprising number of freelancers fail thanks to dehydration. "Those automated guns are big 50-cals. They'll shred a chopper."

"Can you lock them?"

"Someone could get up under them, pull the automatics," I say. "There's still the guards. If there's AK-74s here, who knows what the guards have?"

"Any comms?" Rob asks.

"Not here." I click through a couple menus. "That building there, that's flashing, that's the radio shack. Antenna's up on top of the hill."

"Bingo!" Bradley says. She's holding up a canvas duffel bag. "Look familiar?"

My brow furrows in puzzlement for a second, then I recognize the bag. "Our gear?"

"Looks like it's all here."

Rob straightens and folds his hands together to stretch. His knuckles snap like popcorn. "Then here's the plan."

52

One look in the guard's bathroom and I decide to change clothes out in the security control center. I mean, what is wrong with men? We're in Asia. It's a squat toilet, a pit in the concrete ground, lined with stained white porcelain tile, and they *still* can't hit it.

Noah's house on the other end of the compound probably has gold-laced porcelain thrones. Fat as that bastard is, he probably has someone shake it for him after.

I do wash my hands, though, with a pristine bar of cheap white soap from a tray over the steel sink. I desperately want a bath, even a sponge bath, just to sluice away the Pissed Off Widow pee, but we don't have any time at all. I use my old clothes to wipe the worst of the cave dirt off of me before pulling on the gray-and-green long-sleeve cotton shirt and matching slacks from the duffel bag. Moving's a lot easier with my ribs taped. The mottled bulletproof jacket goes on over that, then my rugged lace-up high-traction dull brown leather boots.

The shiny black leather boots women wear in comic books? Yeah, those are for people who like to get shot.

Bradley's stuffing her gear in her bag while I set three greasy bricks of bitter-smelling plastic explosive around the security control room, each with a short stubby radio detonator sticking out of it. I leave a fourth in the Toilet of What the Hell, Men.

My earpiece buzzes with Rob's voice. "Radio check."

I touch my throat mike. "Ack."

"Yep," Bradley whispers back. She's close enough she's in stereo, once in the earpiece and once right from her lips.

"Doors are ready," Rob says. He's already in quiet mode, barely vocalizing into his mic. We're alone here, but finding our kit changed our practice. We're no longer rats desperately scrabbling at the glass walls of a research lab's tank; we're elite freelance exfiltration professionals, about to deal some serious damage as we exfiltrate ourselves.

My backpack is lighter than it should be. With the broken—sorry, *fractured* ribs, I can't lug a heavy kit bag. I stuff some tools and toys into the cargo pockets of my pants, but even so I have to leave a lot of the gear behind. Explosives are heavy, so I plant a few in the tunnel entrance. I would be the very last person to walk out of that pit, ever. I'm left with a bag I can carry in my left hand without much trouble. My right's free to snatch the long-barrel .38 with the screw-on silencer from the utility belt holster.

Shooting the gun would hurt my ribs, sure. But not as much as letting someone else shoot me.

I still don't like guns. Using a gun means you've screwed up.

We've screwed up.

"Little Beaver, this is Fancypants," Rob's talking into a bulky radio handset.

Bradley rolls to her feet. She snagged a couple of the grenades I couldn't take and clipped them to her belt, and has another .38 semi-auto. Bradley doesn't do silencers.

It's not like one more gunshot is going to attract attention, though.

"Last act is about to start. South end," Rob says in the radio. "Outside the fence." He pauses. "Remain off-stage, out of sight, until my cue. We're taking out the hecklers before your entrance."

My heart is beating quickly again, but it's not fear or stress this time. We're about to go. Maybe we won't kill Noah, but we're sure going to hurt him.

"And four to go," Rob says. He clips the radio to his belt and looks at me. "Beaks, light us up."

I drag my microfiber mask up over my nose and mouth. It feels almost like silk, but lets moisture pass and keeps all sorts of crap out. Combined with the mottled green-and-gray pull-on cap, I look like a movie ninja.

We're ready.

My hands dance across the security controls. "Electric fence down. And…"

My hand pauses over the ENTER key. I don't like killing. No, I *detest* killing. I kill only when I'm not smart enough to avoid it.

But I remember a pair of manacles around my ankles, one chain link ground a quarter of the way through by long-lost hopeless hands. An old tooth, buried in the dirt, knocked from a helpless someone's jaw by forgotten violence. *I don't know who you people were. But I know who dragged you down into those cells, and who dragged you out.*

I hit the key. *This is for you.* "We are live. Sixty seconds."

Rob pulls one of the heavy double doors open, exposing the black night beyond. "Break a leg, ladies."

Bradley leads us out.

53

The Myanmar night is muggy and warm, rich with green growing things and undercut by smoke and oiled metal. The only breeze comes from the cloying insects, so thick that if I didn't have the mask I'd suck them into my lungs with every breath. They batter my eyes, making me blink. I close the security center's reinforced steel door behind us, shutting away the light, and wait for my eyes to accept the darkness.

It's not as black out here as I thought at first. Each of the guard towers has a floodlight beneath the platform, and there's pole lamps every thirty feet or so around the perimeter. I can see the closest fence as an illuminated haze in the darkness, a couple hundred feet away up the side of the mountain, but in front of us, the fence at the bottom and sides is invisible with distance. The damn compound must be a quarter mile across.

Then there's the buildings. The big slumping shape must be the hospital, maybe an oversized Quonset hut, with a light above the closest doors. Further down the slope from us, smaller lights trace walkways through the night between barracks and cottages and everything.

The security control center is this brick blockhouse, a black lurker in the night. The spotty illumination is bright enough to blot out all but the strongest stars.

Forty-five seconds.

I pull the door tight, and hear the lock click into place. Fortunately, I'm tall enough to reach the top of the door easily. I press the stick-on sensor to the very top of the doorframe, where the two doors meet, and hold it there for a count of ten so the glue can set. It's exactly like the one Rob's crew used and I tripped in the access door at Butterfly Star Research. The glue is a lot stronger than the paper holding the sensor together.

When someone opens the door, the paper will tear and trigger the sensor. Which will trigger a whole new sort of hell.

Thirty seconds.

"Ready," I whisper.

Rob, Bradley, and I immediately leave the concrete walkway leading down the hill and veer towards the south, where the light from the belly of a guard tower illuminates the night. We're walking briskly but not running over the smooth, sloping grass. The cameras showed the guards using night vision goggles, and we don't want to worry them too much.

Not for fifteen seconds, anyway.

I know it's coming, but I can't help flinching when the night explodes.

Each guard tower's observation platform has a machine gun mounted beneath it, controlled from the security center. Before leaving, I'd aimed each at the observation platform to its left.

At zero, every one of them fires.

Even at this distance, the sound of that many fifty cals erupting simultaneously feels like a physical pressure, thousands of weak punches from my ears all down my spine. No voice could carry above that tumult, but my brain insists it hears drawn-out shrieks of terror and pain from the observation platforms.

Bradley breaks into a trot. Rob and I follow.

The satchel in my left hand bounces and shakes and rattles at every step, making my shoulder ache and tugging at the ribs on the other side. I should have abandoned more gear, but every tool in the bag feels necessary. If Rob's extraction plan fails we'll have to improvise, quickly and violently. Certainly with a lot of collateral damage.

Rectangles of light appear in the darkness. Exterior lights switch on. We're scurrying through the darkness towards the middle guard tower of the southern fence. The tower's still hammering its neighbor, even as the rounds from its other neighbor chew its superstructure.

Those imaginary screams are lasting longer than any real one could.

A distant mechanical shriek adds its grating tone. Someone's pulled a fire alarm.

Figures start spilling out of the barracks.

My broken ribs burn a little more with each ragged step. I pick up my pace a little more, trying to not let the downhill slope pull me too fast. Any moment now, some poor bastard is going to open the security center door and trip the—

The night explodes behind us.

My shadow suddenly stretches down the hill before me, lingering darkness against the flaring white that vanishes almost before it appears. The ground vibrates beneath my feet, the air quakes. My teeth clatter. My eyes burn.

Maybe I'd used just a *touch* too much plastique?

The blast fills me with its own basso thrum, then recedes.

Another huge crunch vibrates through the ground. The cave entrance collapsing?

The screams are real now, shouts and cries in the darkness behind and below us.

A smoking cannonball of something hits the ground a few yards ahead of us and to the left, the thud of its impact rattling my teeth.

Bradley yells "Shit!" and starts running faster.

Something square hits off on the other side.

It's a ragged chunk of the security center's blockhouse wall, broken and smoldering, half-buried in the grassy ground.

I let my feet take over and start running full-out.

I couldn't carry all those explosives. What was I *supposed* to do with them?

We're another dozen yards down when the dust overtakes us, choking-thick. My mask keeps it out, but my eyes instantly start watering. The lights of the closest guard tower are gone—no, that's not the dust, that's because the machine gun knocked the light off. The guns are silent now.

Between the clunky bag and the busted rib, I'm panting when I approach the skeletal wooden frame of the rickety guard tower. There's a shattered body on the ground just before it, barely visible by the guttering light behind us. Something up the hill's burning, probably ignited by burning debris from the exploding security center.

Bradley beat both Rob and I there. She's already backing away from the nearest fence post, waving us away. I stop about fifty feet away, turn back towards the compound, and squeeze my hands over my ears.

The compound is in glorious chaos. Two of the buildings caught fire, illuminating the pillar of smoke rising from the destroyed security center and the caves beneath it. Distant shadows of people dash from place to place, their collective shouts trumpeting fear and confusion. The stink of concrete dust and burning plastic have overwhelmed the Myanmar jungle, and the fires have drawn a good part of the insects away.

Not a bad night's work for a few chained prisoners.

My stomach knots. It's not a good night's work, either.

Noah's people are experimenting on human beings. That big medical building has a dozen survivors in it and who knows how many buried behind it. They are people, worthwhile human beings, no matter what Noah thinks.

Plus Noah still has his misbegotten booty, all the data from that horrific research. Even if the blast triggered enough power disruptions to destroy the computers holding the medical records, his computer guys will have backed everything up to tape. I suspect that failure to run backups is also a firing squad offense.

And worst of all, Deke is somewhere in that conflagration.

The best part of my heart is with him. I *need* to know how the joy of my life could betray me. How he could turn away from what we had together. How an asshole like Noah could destroy even love.

But Rob looks even worse than my need. He was right: he's getting old. Even with the breathing mask over the lower part of his face, I can see the exhaustion in how he hauls his backpack. He's got his hands over his ears protectively, but his shoulders are slumped. The man's done in.

I'm not letting an old friend—my oldest friend, now—die just to salve my heart.

I will not betray Rob the way Deke betrayed me.

I've lost my love. Rob's husband shouldn't lose his.

But after tonight, Deke will vanish.

I will never find him.

And I have to accept that.

The blast behind us knocks me forward a step, but it's only a sympathetic shockwave. Bradley might not be an explosives guru, but she knows how to blast a hole in a wire fence without bringing the guard tower down on us. She even hung the charge high enough on the pole to not destroy the ground underfoot. There's a little ridge of wire links remaining near the ground, though, high enough that Rob has to step on the steaming hot links to push it low enough for Bradley to step over, so I have to mark her down to a B+. We'll talk.

At least she didn't use the rocket launcher. I know she kept it.

We're running into the cleared zone beyond the fence when I hear the thrum of a chopper. Not a big chopper—one of those little jobs. The thrum has a rhythm, though. It's not purely mechanical—there's music on top of it.

If they're cranking "Ride of the Valkyries," I'll shoot the pilot myself.

There's a brief glimmer in the darkness, a little downhill of us—two quick, almost imaginary flashes, like a firefly against the night.

Rob changes course straight for it. He's dredged up a little strength from somewhere. Bradley hugs his side, ready to catch him. Good.

It's not Wagner.

Creedence, maybe?

Yeah, Creedence. "Run Through the Jungle." That'll do.

The chopper coalesces from the night, this metal bug gleaming in the night, twin runners barely perched on the ground. The rotor's spinning just short of the take-off point—a strong breeze would slip the whole thing down the hill. The pilot's invisible behind the gleaming glass dome of the nose.

The whirling blade is way above my head, but I can't help ducking and holding my head as we charge up to it.

Bradley helps Rob into the gaping door, then hops in herself.

This is it. They're alive.

I'm half-dead.

And once I climb on that chopper, I'll be half-dead forever.

I step on the runner right behind her. "Bradley," I say. "Rob. Thank you for everything." The throat mike carries my words to them even over the rotor wash and Fogarty's wail.

The chopper drifts a foot off the ground, nose towards freedom and safety.

Rob looks at me, half-latched safety straps in his hands.

Knowledge explodes in his eyes.

Before he can say anything, I step off the rail and back onto the killing ground.

54

I graduated from high school when I was fifteen and started in college the next week. I have a doctorate in astrophysics—okay, fine, almost a doctorate. I was ready to defend my thesis when my advisor tried to steal my work and everything went bloody, but that's not the point. I did all the research, all the work. I can even balance my checkbook. I'm smart. I have the paperwork to prove it.

Despite that, what with jumping off the helicopter right before it takes me to safety, all the evidence says I'm a complete idiot.

It's all guesses. Will Rob have the chopper stay? Will he come in after me? Would the pilot even be willing to put down again? Would Bradley insist?

My gut says no. Rob was willing to let me go in alone, to serve as a distraction for Bradley and him. Bradley didn't want this gig, she'd only come along because she owed Rob. The chopper wasn't even vaguely military—who knows where Rob had dug that pilot up, and what leverage and inducements he'd needed to offer?

I need to return to Noah's compound before they can argue it out.

Fortunately, what with the fires burning inside the complex, the crazily tilting floodlights from the shredded guard towers, and the traceries of walkway pole lamps, I can easily find my way back.

The security complex at the high end of the compound is a smoldering red sore in the night, burning (bodies) wood and plastic in a ruptured cyst of shattered concrete blocks. The fire blazing near it must be the building the security system called Supply Shed 3. Further down the hill, the explosion's contagious flames have spread to a low flat roof—the barracks?

Behind me, the sound of the chopper is fading into the night.

I'd guessed right.

They were leaving. Rob couldn't stay, and I'd made my choice.

Bradley'd had her fun, breaking us out.

Now it's my turn.

And I have to be sneaky. One solid punch to the right side of my chest will finish breaking that rib. Probably puncture a lung.

A bouquet of bobbing flashlights blooms where Bradley blew a hole in the fence. I'll need a new way in.

I stop and sink to a knee, catching my breath. My sweat's turning to steam inside the bulletproof jacket. I unzip for a moment, letting the comparatively cool night air flood in. I open my backpack, fumbling to identify each specialized tool by touch.

Some part of me must have known I was going to stay. That's why I kept so much gear.

I clip equipment on my belt, all the way around to the small of my back. The fractured ribs protest when I move my right arm too far or too quickly, so I work carefully and meticulously. Other gear gets slipped into the side pockets of my cargo pants. Night vision goggles wrapped around my head, tilted up but ready to pull into place. I unscrew the silencer, slipping it into a pocket.

I contemplate the throat mike and the earpiece. My team's gone. There's no need to keep them on—there's no reason to keep a radio at all. I can't bring myself to toss them away, though, so I zip them into a small side pocket in the pack.

The backpack's a whole lot lighter now; all the weight's on my belt or in my pockets. I don't have much in the way of hips, but enough that when I cinch the belt another notch the pants aren't going anywhere. I loosen the pack's straps, and with only a few winces get it over my shoulders.

I want to stretch my aching muscles, but with every minute there's a chance Noah's goons might get the mayhem under control. I have to move.

And it's not as simple as diving straight for Deke. Not if I want to live with myself afterwards.

Assuming I live afterwards at all.

No, I got this far. The last thing Noah or his goons will expect is that one of the escapees will sneak back into the complex. Chaos and mayhem are my buddies. I feed them out and they'll watch my back, help me get in and out clean. I study the hillside complex, trying to ignore the way the drifting smoke carries a faint stink of burning flesh.

The uppermost tower on the hillside, the one closest to the security center, fell sometime during the festivities. I don't know how—maybe a flying chunk of concrete took out one of the wooden legs. But without the tower the fence has to be broken, and it's sort of dark. It's certainly a better shot at getting back in than standing by that illuminated fence and snipping my way through the wire.

By the time I pick my way through the broken wood and between spans of snapped fence, my impulse has coalesced into a plan.

55

I find the generators right where the security map said they'd be: at the top of the hill and to the north, great greasy beasts put way out where their chugging won't disturb anyone. The line of lights along the perimeter fence casts faint glimmers across the generators' metal hides. Twin five-hundred-kilowatt Caterpillars, the second ready to leap into action if the first quits, huddling under a four-post aluminum awning. Giant exposed cooling fans that could slice an alligator into julienne fries.

And there's this lovely four-thousand-gallon tank of fuel right next to them. With screw-on gray plastic hoses between the tank and the generators. The hose to the backup generator isn't easy to unscrew, but after a moment of work it comes unstuck and I'm rewarded with the bitter tang of diesel in my nose and cold fuel splashing over my bare hands.

The fuel becomes a glimmering river in the darkness, gushing off the concrete pad and down the hill's hard-packed dirt towards a line of buildings, slump-shouldered in the darkness.

According to the security system, they're supply sheds.

I hope they're wood.

And hold something flammable.

Preferably explosive.

If not explosive, at least all Noah's toilet paper. That would do.

Across the compound and down the hill, distant figures form shadows against the burning security center. Dancing flashlights reveal people running across the ground, little cliques dashing for each guard tower. Worse for me, the fire atop the barracks is going out. Tiny men are forming into squads and heading out in selected directions. My infectious chaos is dying, the antibodies of Noah's organization marshaling themselves.

Did that platoon way down in front of the barracks start to head towards me? It's hard to tell—there's only a little puddle of light down there, and the thugs getting instructions only stand for a minute before heading out.

I make myself wait a minute.

What is the speed of diesel flowing over broken dry ground, anyway?

No, I can't wait any more. If that crew isn't on their way up here, another crew is. I leave a small bit of explosives, just a puppy charge really, at the bottom of the diesel tank and start trotting into the darkness.

Fuel tanks don't explode. They just burn, unless you get the mixture of air and fuel just right. Still, it's really hard to hold myself to a trot as I cross the face of the hill, heading back towards the burning security center.

After the security center detonation and blasting our way through the fence, the crack-snap of the puppy charge barely registers. The massive *foomph* of igniting diesel pushes at my back, but it fades before I can stop and look.

A river of fire courses down the hill. It didn't reach the supply buildings, though. Too bad.

It did catch the half-dozen people standing near it by surprise, though. Silhouetted against the flame, they're stumbling backwards, arms raised to ward off the fire. One person's running flat-out downhill, panicked, his rifle in an upraised hand.

Thank you, Chaos.

It's maybe another two seconds before traceries of walkway lights, the line of illuminated fence, and the rectangular gleam of windows all go dark simultaneously. There's a few more shouts in the darkness, mingled anger and frustration, all leavened with a healthy dose of fear. Like so many supposedly secure organizations, their contingency plans all relied on a single uncrackable nut—and we'd cracked it first thing. The idiots had locked it behind us. Some of the shouts are in English, others in that liquid tonal tongue.

Gunshot! My feet want to jerk myself into motion, but my eyes haven't adjusted to the deeper darkness yet. Only a distant bark, probably panic fire. Instead of moving, I slide my night vision goggles over my eyes and turn them on low.

The burning pit of the security center is suddenly a white glaring sun. So is the generator shed behind me. The buildings become shadowy cubes and curves against the cooling earth, with the hot green shapes of people scattering between them. More modern goggles would give me smoother images and a greater range of contrast, but these are what Rob could scrounge up in whatever Naypyidaw market he and Bradley hit.

Two groups, maybe a dozen people all told, are running up towards the generator. I start my own trot in a curving arc down to the oversized inverted half-tube of Noah's research hospital.

With the night vision goggles it's easy enough to avoid Noah's thugs. I'm careful not to surge away from any of the people my goggles pick out, though.

I'm certain Noah equipped some of his thugs with night vision goggles of their own. The watchers in the guard towers surely had them. And I'd seen a whole wall rack stuffed with goggles in the security center. The last thing I needed was for some bright boy with a pair of night eyes he'd snuck into the barracks to look up the hill and say "Hey, that person's sneaking around everyone."

But I get to the hospital easily enough.

The hospital's walls are corrugated aluminum, just as they looked from a distance, and even at two in the morning they radiate the day's heat against my fingers and palm. I follow the rippling wall along to one end, find the door, and slip inside.

When the hospital's heavy door clicks shut behind me, it blocks out all the shouting and clanging and even the stenches of smoke and ash. The air feels cool and clean as I pull it in, without even a faint hint of sickness or antiseptic. My sweat quickly turns clammy and sludgy, and I can't help shivering just a little. That aluminum wall must be two layers, with some heavy insulation in between them.

According to the security center map, the rooms on either side of me are the datacenter, while straight ahead the hospital fills the main part.

Sniff. Is that citrus?

I adjust the night vision goggles, increasing their sensitivity until I can make out the shape of the walls around me and the doors down the corridor. This part of the world probably hasn't had this much cool air in one place since the last Ice Age, if then. Maybe since Pangea. If Noah's goons snatch experimental victims from the surrounding villages, they must think they've died and gone to Antarctica instead of Hell.

I slip forward. With all the mayhem outside, right now is the best chance to escape those poor people in here will ever get.

If they can walk. If they can make it to the river, to the boats. If they can drive the boats. In the dark.

I can't fix everything.

Unlike the outer door, the door leading further in is locked. I don't recognize the model but it's a simple thing, probably a push-button on the other side, meant for home use. I pull my (beautiful!) lock picks from a pocket and, working by touch, pop the lock in less than a minute.

I gently ease the door open an inch.

Sing-song voices, low and urgent.

A flicker of light crosses the door. Moves on.

I flip the night vision goggles up. The full-featured goggles we'd had in

Portugal, or even the ones I'd had back at Butterfly Star, would handle a flashlight beam just fine. If someone spotlit me here, though, these cheap knock-offs would blind me.

Someone's speaking short and sharp—giving orders? I don't even know which language they're babbling in, how am I supposed to guess? He shuts up, and people start moving, so it must have been orders.

Someone's crying—not loud bawling, but the slow and constant huffing for breath that means they've been crying for a long time and don't have any reason to stop.

With everything going wrong outside, I wouldn't put it past Noah to order the subjects killed.

My .38 semi-auto is suddenly in my hand. I pull a little flashlight out of a pocket and hold it in my left, ready to flick it on if needed.

Heart pounding, I nudge the door open and slip through.

It's a cavernous room, longer than it is wide. I'm standing amidst a flotilla of ancient wheelchairs. Decrepit gurneys stand with their heads near the walls and feet toward the middle, creating a corridor big enough for four or five people to walk in formation. A rolling cart with dark computer monitors and medical equipment sits by each.

Near the middle of the room—in the spotty light, at first I think they're zombies.

Most of Noah's victims have shambled out of bed. They're holding on to the edges of their gurneys and convenient but rickety chairs. One still struggles with his—her?—sheets.

One woman stands strong, an electric lantern in her upraised left hand. She erupts with another liquid string of orders, and the broken wrecks struggle to obey.

I've seen healthier-looking folks in photos of concentration camp survivors.

Lantern light flashes off something in the woman's right hand. Peering, I can make out the angular metallic shape of a handgun.

What is she doing? Taking these poor bastards outside before she shoots them?

Rage burns in my gut. It's all I can do to not pull the trigger right there.

But I can't be sure of killing her in one shot.

I can't see how she's holding the handgun, or even what kind it is. Is her finger outside the guard or on the trigger? Automatic, semi-auto, or revolver?

If her hand clamps down in death, someone might get hurt.

I raise the flashlight in one fist and the gun in the other. I have to concentrate on which to trigger first. My light's a small LED thing, but it's strong enough to put a halo of light on her black hair. "Move and I shoot you."

The woman freezes.

So do the shambling skeletons around the room.

Terrified faces peer in my direction. I'm invisible to them, other than maybe a vague shape behind a dot of light.

"You with the gun," I say. "Turn around. Slow."

Holding the lantern high, the woman shuffles to face me.

It's Pissed Off Widow.

56

Pissed Off Widow doesn't have a measly handgun, either. The edge of my flashlight's illumination brushes the boxy shape of a machine pistol in her hand. That thing can blast more rounds in a second than my .38 can hold. It looks like her finger's outside the trigger guard, not on the trigger, and she's pointing it at the hospital's concrete floor, so that's something.

But in the hospital's freakishly citrus-scented cold darkness, with the wheezing and trembling victims of Noah's experimentation surrounding her, I can't be sure of killing her before she fountains death.

And if she recognizes me behind this flashlight, she'll accept death if it means killing me.

I try to make my voice lower pitched and slower than usual. "Drop the gun."

Pissed Off Widow stares unblinking at my light. She licks her lips nervously.

"Do it!" I shout.

"Is wrong!" Pissed Off Widow's voice trembles with passion. "These people, they do nothing!"

I'm gobsmacked.

"You keep them here?" She raises her chin in defiance. "You shoot me."

I've interrupted a rescue.

How can I be on the same side as a woman who dumped a bucket of her own pee on me?

My flashlight wobbles.

Pissed Off Widow's gun hand twitches.

I snap, "Don't move!"

My gut clenches—I didn't disguise my voice that time.

She says, "Shoot." I've seen people ready to die before. She's not bluffing. "Or do not shoot. I take them."

My heart thuds in my throat. I remember to drop my voice, this time. "Go out the other door."

The lantern dips a little. She peers, trying to see past my flashlight.

"The docks are still okay," I say.

"Boats are stupid," Pissed Off Widow says. "We take truck."

Why's a boat stupid? And what kind of trucks do they have? "Fine. Don't go by this end of the hospital, or by the cottages."

"Why?" she says.

Deepen my voice. "Go quickly. No time. Run."

Pissed Off Widow studies my shadow. "These people—my husband only wanted work. He died. You kill." She bares her teeth. "Kill *everybody*."

A clot of acid burns my gut. She probably thinks her husband's murderer burned to death in the explosion, or maybe got buried alive. It's the only break I'm getting here. "Hurry! Five minutes!"

Pissed Off Widow turns to the skeletal survivors and shouts in her own language. They lurch back into motion, faster this time. One of them helps the gaunt woman trapped in her own sheets.

I walk backwards, retreating towards the door I came in. There's a little suicidal part of me that wants to tell her the truth, that her husband hadn't said horrible things about her before she died. Another part wants to lie to her again, and tell her that her husband's last words had been of her.

In another life, we might have been friends.

Instead, I slip back into the hallway and lock the door behind me. I leave one of my less useful picks jammed into the mechanism, so she can't unlock the door from within. I'll grab it on my way out, before blowing the next brick of explosives.

The lock on the left-hand computer room is easier to pick. It's an office, though. The flashlight reveals the debris of a typical IT crew: trash of abandoned computer parts scattered over desks, haphazard papers. An open storage cabinet overflows with half-dismantled machines. Without ventilation, it's obvious that the computer crew's body odor infected the cloth-covered office chairs. The only things missing are the empty pizza boxes and cola bottles—no, I take that back, there's a cardboard box that started off holding reams of paper, now overflowing with repulsively sticky cans of Chinese cola.

The door across the hall has a biometric keypad and a knob lock. Much more likely candidate. The keypad gleams to life when I touch it—there's a battery backup. Unlike the mechanisms in Noah's home, though, this security system keeps its brains on the outside. I need about two minutes to short it out, release the bolt, and slip the cover back on. Another thirty seconds to pick the mechanical lock.

I've been in small datacenters, but this one qualifies as "snug." There's three racks of equipment wedged up against the curved wall, still gleaming in my night vision goggles, with barely enough space in front of them for a person to work. A half-height metal cabinet serves as makeshift monitor stand, but there's no room for a chair. I smell static electricity and hot plastic.

I don't want to believe that these few racks of equipment suffice to contain the records of so much human misery. They ought to ooze gore or something.

I barely shut the datacenter door behind me when the wall vibrates.

A masculine voice shouts angry orders.

Feet tromp.

They've found me.

57

I'm in no shape to fight. My side aches from fractured ribs, and the duct tape Bradley used to stabilize them itches like crazy. I have a third-hand handgun with a twelve-shot magazine and one in the chamber, plus enough plastic explosive to make a suicide vest worthy of the name. No partners, no backup, and no extraction plan.

And I'm locked in a coat closet used as a datacenter.

So it's flight.

The infrared goggles show the outside wall arching up into the ceiling, meeting the interior wall maybe twelve feet overhead. The air conditioning ducts are pitch black shafts, still oozing cold even half an hour after I've cut the power. They're big enough for a beagle, but not a basset.

There's no back door.

Flight is out.

Which leaves—hide.

The three jam-packed server racks are wedged up against the wall. A waist-high metal cabinet, far too small to hide in, with a twenty-inch flat screen precariously balanced on it. The server racks still glow red, above human body temperature. The heat rising from them clashes against the cool air sinking from the air duct, which these cheap night-vision goggles interpret as midair rippling.

If I climb those racks, anyone with a flashlight or night vision goggles will pick me right up.

Wait—the wall is curved. The tops of the server racks are right up against the wall, but putting something square up against a curve leaves a little bit of room. Just a little.

I scuttle over to the cabinet, trying to keep my steps quiet.

Someone shouts in the hall. There's a rattle. The datacenter doorknob?

I'm sweating again. My hands want to shake. I don't let them.

Once I finish here, when I take care of Noah's abominable research, I'm free to reach Deke with a clear conscience. Maybe take out Noah in the bargain.

All I have to do is live that long.

Yes—there's a gap behind the cabinets. I don't have time to look further. I plop onto my butt, flinching as my ribs complain, and stick my feet into the space.

I slide in easily up to my knees, and press on.

Something catches my right foot.

My foot can bend around it—a computer cable. The kind of computer techs who heap rancid cola cans in their office usually leave a nightmare tangle of wires behind their servers.

I twist my foot. The cable snags on my waffle-tread boots, but finally slips off my toes.

Another shout in the hall. A snapped order in response.

I scoot back, my feet striking cable after cable. I twist and kick until they slip free.

In another moment I'm wedged behind the racks, squeezed against the curved aluminum wall. Even with the mask over my face, the dusty must of neglected spaces fills my nose. Cables have knotted uncomfortably around my calves and thighs. I'm sure I unplugged more than one machine and yanked out more than one cable. If this machine room was live, I would have set off a dozen alarms, but now, cables snaring me in but good is my only worry.

And being found. There's that worry, too.

I rest my weight on my left elbow, and keep the .38 handy in my right, finger over the trigger guard. The equipment on my belt and in my pockets digs and gouges at my body.

One of those pains in my pants pocket is a silencer. Using the silencer might help me hide for a moment, but if I'm still screwing it on when the door opens, I'm either dead or taken alive.

If someone looks back here, I'll shoot them in the face.

That'll mean my death, sure.

But so far, tonight's score is a whole bunch to nothing, Beaks versus everyone. I've snuck in like Catwoman. I've taken out everyone I came up against. I made sure Noah's victims had a chance for escape.

My lips twitch up. I could complain, but nobody likes a sore winner.

The datacenter door flings open, stopping only when it bangs against the wall.

My hint of a smile vanishes.

My finger slips off the trigger guard, onto the trigger.

A heavy-duty flashlight beam plays around the room, bouncing off the aluminum exterior wall. I squint against the reflection. If I'd been wearing the night vision goggles, I'd be blind.

The person in the doorway says a single word.

The datacenter door slams.

I don't dare breathe.

Instead, I listen. More commands in the hallway, but I try to hear past them for the scuff of boots on concrete. The wheeze of breath or the click of knees. Any little sound that means someone's standing in the datacenter with me.

Nothing.

I gently release the breath I've been holding.

There's a heavy thud.

Something snaps and cracks.

A distant scream of rage. A sound like tearing canvas.

My guts instantly turn to liquid. I'm pushing my head to the floor, my cheek hugging the cool concrete, even as bullets punch through the interior wall and split the air overhead.

Screams, cut off short.

Over my head, bullets ping off the server rack. Metal pops as more bullets punch through the aluminum walls.

In the hall, someone shouts "Beaks! Beaks!"

It takes me a moment to put it together.

A search party found the locked hospital door. They kicked it open.

Pissed Off Widow opened fire.

And the goons think she's me.

I should thank her for the diversion.

Plus, when everything goes to hell, Noah's people blame me. The thought makes me smile.

One bullet of many smacks the floor three inches from my face.

Concrete chips fly.

Pain slashes through my left cheek.

58

The sideways hail of bullets cuts off.

In the hallway outside the datacenter, men are screaming. Shouting.

Boots pound concrete. Shoulders rattle the walls.

Guns bark, much more loudly than the last ones. They're deeper, too, and further apart. Probably Noah's goons with AK-74s.

The gunfire gets more numerous, moving into the hospital proper.

Pissed Off Widow's machine pistol responds, but it's a quick burst.

I scoot forward, thrashing myself free of the frustrating cables tangled around my legs. Still on my side, I squirm around to the front of the metal storage cabinet.

The cabinet's sides feel heavy. It's fireproof, or at least fire-resistant. Probably steel. I want to stay low, but keeping my thighs and legs behind the server rack while opening the cabinet means lying on my fractured ribs, and that is *not* happening. Heart pounding in my throat and fresh sweat on my spine, I squirm out from behind the cabinet and sit cross-legged in front of the cabinet. Head squeezed as far between my shoulders as possible, waiting for the bullets to cut the air again, I start on the lock.

Thirty eternal seconds later, the lock gives.

The flashlight reveals rows of backup tapes, each smaller than half a pack of cards. A computer-printed label is meticulously affixed to each.

A proper operation would keep backups off-site. But no storage company is going to drive out to the Myanmar jungle to swap tapes documenting immoral and illegal research on humans.

I scan the labels. Daily backups, who cares? Weekly, monthly, maybe.

More gunfire. Are the soldiers moving on?

A short hard *clang*. A stray bullet punctures the air.

I don't have time to lie flat. Not now.

There, at the bottom! PROJECT A FINAL. PROJECT B FINAL. All the way up to Project R.

I'm sure every one of those projects would knot my stomach and send me running for a flamethrower, but I don't have time for revulsion. I open my backpack and scoop every tape in.

The rifle fire stops.

The thugs outside are moving on.

Pissed Off Widow must be getting away. And taking Noah's henchmen with her.

I silently wish her well, toss last weekend's backup tapes on top of my loot, then zip the bag shut. Slipping it over my shoulders pulls a thin line of pain from my busted ribs.

If Noah's victims are still here, they're dead.

And I'll move faster without so much plastic explosive, anyway.

I stuff three bricks into the middle server rack, right on top of a bulky storage array. Ready the timer and the detonator.

That leaves me with one brick. I don't have plans for it, but a bit of plastique is a good thing to have. I fiddle with the brick and my last detonator, then jam the assembly into a thigh pocket.

The building still echoes with gunfire, but it's distant. A remote shout echoes through the hall, but it's muffled by distance as well as the door.

This is as good a chance as I'm going to have.

I set the timer for two minutes and slip out the door.

The hallway is a meat grinder. The corpses of four men lie crumpled about. Even in the dim firelight reflecting through the open exterior door, the floor gleams with fresh blood. Another man lies on his side, groaning, holding his guts. Buzzing insects already slip in through the open door to flock around their coppery meals.

I stoop to seize a dead man's assault rifle as I walk past. My fingers find the improved safety that tells me it's one of the AK-74M series, the final model made before the Soviet Union fell. It's a modern AK-47, basically indestructible. I grab two thirty-round magazines, squeezing the extra ammunition into the thigh pocket I just emptied of plastique.

I'm not liking guns any more. But in this madness, anyone *without* an assault rifle is conspicuous.

As I walk towards the outside door, the dying man raises a gore-covered hand.

I want to say that his death, all these deaths, is Noah's fault. Or Pissed Off Widow's fault.

But if I hadn't returned, he would have lived. Facing this dying man, I'm hard-pressed to weigh the wrecks from the hospitals against him.

I'm not strong enough to look at his face before walking past.

His feebly clutching hand falls short of my calf.

I tromp through his life blood and escape with only another stab wound in my soul.

Outside doesn't feel any cleaner. The security center is a pit of superheated cinders, casting a pillar of gleaming embers into the night. The diesel generators still burn, but that fire has spread to the supply sheds, and their bright yellow radiance far outshines everything else. Another guard tower has started burning, too—I have no idea why or how. The smoke has driven away some of the bugs, but enough remains that I'd choke if I uncovered my mouth.

Gunfire explodes: AK-74s, with the occasional burst from a machine pistol. Pissed Off Widow is still at it, and I'm betting she's not any happier.

A distant motor roars. The mysteriously burning guard tower shudders.

The exit's right by that tower. And from the sound of shooting, so are most of Noah's thugs. I send Pissed Off Widow and the escaping victims a kind thought and start down the hill. With so much random light I don't dare risk my cheap-ass night vision goggles, so I can only walk briskly rather than run.

The fires make the line of sturdy cottages rolling down towards the water stand out just a little against the darkness. They look like they're ripped from a New England seaside town—broad planks painted a glossy white or yellow or pale green, tight double-hung windows, all maybe twenty feet on a side and identical. Probably pre-manufactured. It must have cost Noah a fortune to get them to the back end of nowhere.

I'm not running. Nobody's shooting at me. The AK-74 slung over my left shoulder clunks against my hip. I reholster my .38 so I can hold the rifle steady. Firing this beast will murder my ribs, but that's better than getting murdered by someone else. If it was another type of rifle, I wouldn't even consider shooting it, but the AK-74 has surprisingly little recoil. The slope starts to level out, moving towards the river plain.

But my heart's throbbing like I was climbing a mountain. My sweat isn't just from the summer heat of a Myanmar midnight.

The security system said that Deke had the last cottage in the row.

Maybe he's moved on, to Japan or Australia or wherever.

Maybe he's out with the thugs shooting at Pissed Off Widow.

No. My pride flares. If Deke was out there, Pissed Off Widow would be dead and buried by now.

Another guard tower, down by the river, suddenly flickers with flame. Not my doing—she must have prepared her own diversions before rescuing the hospital prisoners.

Yeah, we could have been friends. In another life.

That's not the point.

I don't want to think about the point.

Deke's not going to stay in his assigned quarters when the hellhounds have broken their chains and are setting fire to the place. But maybe I can find evidence. Hints.

Something to tell me how he turned on me.

Because if it's as simple as *Noah paid me enough*, I will never trust anyone again.

Not for the rest of my life.

And I don't know if I can live knowing that.

Deke's wooden cottage is painted glossy white, with bright red trim, on a brick foundation, maybe fifty feet from the docks beside the rushing river.

Give it a picket fence and I'll set it on fire. Depending on what's inside, I might set it on fire anyway.

The cottage's front door's ajar, maybe two inches.

A steady gleam of electric light shines through the gap. I catch hints of light at the edges of the tightly drawn drapes.

My hands are shaking. My tangled feelings explode from my soul, seeming to knot themselves around my every muscle. My bowels knot, my head trembles.

Deke must have left the door open when he ran out.

I tap the muzzle of the AK-74 against the door.

It creaks open another inch.

Knot in my throat.

I can't breathe.

It takes every scrap of my will to jab the door hard enough to swing it open.

A tilted platform looms in the middle of the room. It's a medieval torture wheel, built of splintery wood.

A naked man lies spread-eagle on it, manacled to the edges.

He bears brutal gunshot wounds in his arms and legs. Coarse black thread knots the wounds shut, but flies have accumulated in the seeping sores surrounding them.

Starvation has ravaged his muscles. His ribs are a xylophone.

There's another gunshot wound on his cheek, savagely stitched, but the infection's bad enough to swell the eye above it shut.

He somehow finds the strength to open the other eye.

Focus on me.

"Whoever you are," Deke wheezes through broken teeth. "Please. Kill me."

59

I still can't breathe.

But now I can't move either.

Except for the tremble that's claimed every muscle. That won't stop.

The sight of Deke's ruined body, chained up for display like discount baked ham in a questionable deli's second-rate cooler, shatters me.

He hadn't turned against me.

The knowledge I'd uncovered in Noah's home computer was true. Deke had spilled his guts—while drugged. A little Dilaudid will loosen anyone's tongue.

Especially if they're painfully maimed.

But the context—*Mr. Don Eckhart's enthusiastic cooperation continues unabated*—had been a lie.

Noah had learned everything through torture.

But I'd believed that he'd turned.

I hadn't trusted that he loved me the way I loved him.

That he would *never* turn.

I was the one who'd betrayed Deke.

Deke's eyes sag hopelessly shut, but he tries, "Parlez-vous francais?" in his Georgia drawl.

My brain burns like a sun inside my skull. I need to shout with joy and grovel for forgiveness. All I can say is, "Your French accent is still crap, Deke."

I might as well have run one-ten volts through him. Deke's eye snaps wide and he thrashes against the chains. Dark blood oozes from new-ruptured wounds around the manacles. "Billie! What're you doing here?"

"Saving your hide." I slam the door behind me and pull the grungy microfiber mask down off my nose and chin. Sweat puffs off my face like steam.

The cottage is mostly one large room, with a corner cut out for the bathroom. There's no cottage furniture here, though. Deke's rack dominates, but a few folding tables stand against the walls. There's a little glass-doored dorm fridge with clinically clean clear glass vials. A trap door leading to the cottage's crawlspace. A folding chair, a decrepit wheelchair. Two more folding chairs around a collapsible card table.

An abused wooden dining room table just next to Deke holds orderly stacks of clean bandages. Bottles of painkillers stand marshalled for inspection, everything from aspirin and acetaminophen to hard narcotics. Another line of bottles presents antibiotics, penicillin and Cipro and Z-Pacs. An engraved silver platter of bananas, kiwis, and dragonfruit has attracted its own cloud of flies. A clear glass pitcher of water with a spotless glass beside it. Pristine white sweatpants and a cotton T-shirt, neatly folded. All spotlighted by a battery-driven emergency fixture in the ceiling.

Unchained, Deke could grab any of it just by sitting up.

My self-loathing ignites into pure anger.

That's *it*.

Noah *needs* death.

"Spilled my guts," Deke's stare is feral, like he's ready to eat me up. Like he'd surrendered himself to the Reaper and had never expected to see me again.

"I know." I pick up the pitcher and sniff it. The same chlorinated water I'd had earlier. I focus on pouring a glassful. "How do you think we found you? Here, drink this."

Deke eagerly sips. I get half a glass in him before pulling back. "Not too much. You can't throw up, not now. Let me get these locks."

"You can't get me out," Deke says. His voice is thicker now—the water's loosened whatever gunk's accumulated in his throat.

"I am Billie Carrie fucking Salton." I snatch my picks and attack the manacle at Deke's left wrist. "I get *everything* out. Including you."

Everything has changed.

My complete lack of an extraction plan hadn't worried me. Chances were I wouldn't need it.

But extraction is now *everything*.

Maybe, if I can get Deke out of here, maybe I can make it up to him.

Make up for not trusting him.

"Who all's with you?"

"Just me." I bite my lip in concentration. The lock isn't more difficult than mine, but my hands want to shake. "Rob and Bradley had to bail."

"You can't get me out alone," Deke repeats with a wheeze.

"Shut up," I hiss, twisting my picks. "I am *not* giving up on you again."

The manacle's lock isn't much better than the ones in the caves.

But when it snaps open, the smell is terrible. Deke fought the manacles until he lost his strength, and the wounds have swelled red with infection. And Noah's left Deke here the whole time. Given him enough medical treatment and IV fluids to keep him just this side of death. Taunted him with painkillers and antibiotics and all the other things that would help him heal.

Deke groans. Bending his elbow splashes a grimace across his face. He's clearly running on the sudden shock of adrenaline, burning his final reserves of strength.

I free his other wrist. Deke's whole body sags, supported by his splayed legs. If the wooden platform didn't have that thirty degree back-tilt, he would collapse forward. I kneel to attack the manacle around his left ankle. "When I get this open, let's get your foot on the ground. Let the table take your weight."

Deke nods. That red scabby scar in his handsome cheek is awful.

Noah will die. *Screaming.*

And I will laugh.

I can't think about that. Not right now. I need to get this lock open, not quiver in rage.

The ankle manacle slipping open rips a gasp from Deke. More infection swells the ankle, intensified by the weight of his body resting against the rough-forged iron. "It's okay," I say, guiding his foot to the gleaming golden-stained pine plank floor. I've hoisted Deke before, during hand-to-hand practice. He must have lost half his weight. My ribs still shriek as I guide his bulk, but I don't dare show it. Deke can't know I'm hurt, or he'll get all noble on me.

My poor Deke sobs as his last foot comes free. He's still leaning on the torture platform, but he's got both bare feet on the varnished floorboards.

"Can you hold a glass?" I ask.

Deke's hands shake like he's sixty years older, but he manages a double grip around it.

"Not too fast," I say, and attack the medical supplies.

First, he needs a painkiller. Not enough to put him out, just enough so he can move without screaming. Ibuprofen and Norco won't do—they're pills, I don't want to put anything in his gut right now. I'll stick some acetaminophen up the wrong end if I have to. ("Hi Deke! Bend over and spread them for me!" Oh, *that'll* go over well.)

But the little fridge has morphine. I scan the label for the concentration, take a guess at Deke's body weight, draw a few milligrams into a syringe, and stab it into a pale blue vein.

In only seconds, Deke relaxes. He doesn't quite sag to the floor, but the mortal tension in his every muscle fades just a little. I don't dare give him more, I'll never move him without his help. But his eyes clear, just a little.

A massive dose of injectable ciproflaxin follows—the sooner we start fighting that infection the better. That high a dose might cause tendon damage, but we'll worry about that tomorrow.

The bandages aren't just gauze. Noah stocked up on instant-coagulation wraps—the real Israeli ones, not the cheap knock-offs. They're meant for fresh wounds, but they'll help with the slow seeping serum from Deke's injuries and the oozing scabs I've broken.

Deke smells like old cheese about to go bad.

Maybe I'll let Noah live until I get tired of hearing him scream.

That might take a long time.

I'll shatter Noah's empire. Donate everything he treasures to causes more worthy than him. Like the Pederast Priest Legal Defense Fund.

The pants aren't strictly necessary for escape, except that they are. Deke's barely holding on to life, and the surge of strength the hope of escaping's given him can't last. I can't have Deke distracted by his willy getting chomped by mosquitoes, and a hit of dignity might ease him as much as the morphine did. Lifting each leg to slip the sweatpants over his feet detonates my ribs again, painfully enough that I have to hold my breath so Deke doesn't catch a stray whimper.

The T-shirt's a lot easier.

"Looking good," I say, grabbing the wheelchair. "Your ride, sir."

Deke tries to help. It's better than doing a dead lift, but only just. The pain grays my vision before I get him in place.

Once Deke's in place I lean against the wheelchair, eyes closed, panting for a moment. My ribs hurt—everything hurts.

The pain is a distraction.

I hate to do it, but I grab the bottle of Norco. It's the great big chunky pills. I break one in half so it'll take effect more quickly and chase the halves with a swig of water. Yes, the opiate will make me a little fuzzy—but the pain is covering me in fuzz. I'll come out ahead. The rest of the bottle goes in the thigh pocket recently vacated by explosives.

My Deke looks pitiful, huddled on the scarred and torn plastic seat, his feeble arms clearly inadequate to the wheels. His working eye still hasn't stopped staring at me. I bend over him to fasten the flimsy worn polyester lap belt, but the buckle's long gone.

"It's too much," he whispers in my ear. "You'll never make it out with me." Deke's breath smells terrible. I can't get enough of it. I stay bent close just for a moment, so I can feel his exhalation on my cheek.

"I'm rescuing you. Shut up."

I take a moment to breathe him in, and when I'm not paying attention the words escape. "My mother. You told them about my mother."

Deke blinks. "Found her that day. That last day. Was going to tell you after."

A knot loosens in my heart.

But there's no time for my heart.

The AK-74's still on the floor. Still bent by him, I say, "Think you can handle a thirty-eight?"

"For you?" The unmaimed side of Deke's face twists in that treasured grin. "I'll jump sideways, through the air, shootin' two guns."

That smile, even only half of it, softens just a little of the horrible pain in my soul.

Deke hadn't turned.

Maybe he'll even forgive me, eventually. But I'll have to tell him first.

I pull off my backpack and stuff it into his lap, then I unclip the holster from my belt and slip the weapon into his hands. "Full magazine, one in the chamber."

"Let's rock," he whispers in my ear.

Pulling away from Deke aches like pulling a tooth.

But it's time to get out of here.

I kneel to grab the AK-74.

When I stand, the curtained window beside the front door shatters.

And a tactical nuke explodes in the middle of my back.

60

Blinding pain shatters out from my spine, splintering my every thought into jagged shards.

My cheek hurts too.

I taste blood. More blood clogs my nose.

What's under me quivers—

It's floor. Varnished wooden floor.

A heavily-booted foot lands an inch from my eye. My other eye is pressed against a floorboard.

My butt is in the air. Arms splayed to the sides.

Total lack of dignity.

The boot swings away.

I close my eye and wait for the kick.

Instead, metal clatters across wood.

I try to breathe. Gotta get myself together.

Fire lights up my back. Did I break even *more* ribs?

It takes Deke's pained groan to slap me into actual consciousness.

I'm on the cabin floor, face-down beside the torture wheel, right on my busted cheekbone. An angry mule has kicked me in the middle of my back.

No, not a mule.

A *bullet*.

I've been shot.

A bulletproof vest doesn't deflect bullets. It just spreads out the impact. Instead of getting punctured with a half-inch steel slug, it's like being bludgeoned with a two-foot-wide battering ram.

I'm hurt.

"Do say you're still with us, Miss Salton."

I know that voice, oozing with bogus charm.

It's Jack Noah.

I want to leap up and tear his throat out with my teeth. But I'm barely conscious. Even anger feels out of reach.

Can I feel my feet? I cautiously wiggle my right big toe within its boot. My cotton-covered toes brush smooth steamy leather. The left toe works, too.

The shot didn't sever my spine. The bulletproof vests Rob got us might not have been top-of-the-line, but I'll never knock last year's model again. I probably have the worst bruise of my life. I'll be lucky if more ribs didn't break.

The boot tromps back into view, an arm's length from me this time. Stops.

Parts of myself click back together. I'm lying on my face, in front of the man who murdered my friends, tortured Deke, and planned to use me as a lab rat. I don't know what's going to happen, but I do know that I'm meeting it on my feet.

I shift my weight forward, trying to straighten my legs and get my hands under me. My back shrieks in protest.

"Oh, good," Noah says. "I'm so delighted my newest employee didn't die on her first day."

At first I'm not sure I heard him correctly. Then I spasm past the pain, convulsing forward and rolling onto my back, left hand holding me up and right scrabbling at my belt for my semi-auto.

It's gone.

My eyes throw everything else aside to find Deke first. He's in the wheelchair, huddled over. I can only see his swollen-shut eye… but I think he's crying.

Maybe Noah didn't *turn* Deke.

But he looks completely broken.

"Now, now, Miss Salton," Noah says. He's standing just inside the cabin's open door, wearing blousy green cotton pants, a matching long-sleeved shirt tucked into his belt, and a veiled hat like a beekeeper. Clouds of insects flow around him, drawn into the little cottage by the battery-powered ceiling light.

The taste of blood in my throat gets a lot stronger. Sitting propped on one hand, my back stops shrieking in exchange for an unending wail of aching complaint.

The threatening boot belongs to a little Asian woman. If I was standing, she might come up to my busted rib. Unlike most of Noah's thugs, she's dressed all in black, in this ridiculous skintight "hey look at my tits" catsuit. Hair pulled so tightly back it had to hurt. Shiny black leather boots, just right for reflecting lights and attracting attention. From the ground, though, her silver automatic pistol looks as big as a bazooka. She doesn't seem to blink, just keeps the gun aimed right between my eyes and her finger right on the trigger.

The metallic contents of my pockets dig at my legs. Some of them might be useful, if I could reach them without getting shot.

And just because I can feel my toes doesn't mean I can stand, or walk, or anything complicated like that.

I say, "I'm—" and the one word triggers a spasm of coughing.

When I got shot, I hit my nose on the floor. I don't think it's broken, but blood trickles over my upper lip.

"Don't be tedious, woman." Noah raises his chin. "You're smarter than that. Deke is your salary. You've cost me a great deal." Noah crosses his flabby arms over his bulging gut. "It's only right you should compensate me for it."

Another cough clears my throat. "You want me to make it up to you?"

"You clearly misunderstand capitalism," Noah says. "I *own* you now, Salton. You and Eckhart both. My varied business interests have many inconvenient competitors. You'll… handle them for me. That's what you like doing, isn't it? Taking down big companies? Harming their stockholders? You'll keep doing that. But now… you do it for me."

The idea revolts me, even as my brain lurches to create a plan. But I don't dare twitch while under the woman's guard. Her eyes have not moved, and she's clearly ready to plant two rounds between my eyes.

"Let's spare the obvious arguments," Noah says. "You'll say you'd rather die. That's unfortunate. But no matter what you choose, Eckhart lives. Your only negotiating point is the conditions which he endures. Perform well enough, and I'll bring in a physical therapist to help him walk again—per diem, of course. Perform poorly, and I'll send him back for more of Miss Xi's tender ministrations. And better performance means better conditions for you: better hotels, first-class travel."

Deke looks even more decrepit than the wheelchair he's huddling in. I can't believe he's going to live through the night, let alone another day.

But Noah has the facilities to keep Deke's breath nailed to his flesh. I blew up the hospital datacenter, but I'm sure there's medical supplies elsewhere. And Noah's just the sort of asshole who would spend exorbitant funds to keep a victim alive just to taunt a dead woman.

I try to swallow, but my mouth is bone-dry.

"That's the negotiation," Noah says. His voice is insufferable with victory. "Either the next words out of your mouth are 'I agree,' or Miss Xi here puts two bullets between your ears and resumes her personal charge of Eckhart."

Trapped. My choices are all horrific.

"Come now," Noah says. "I don't have all night."

I select the least appalling option.

The words taste like vomit. "I agree."

Noah gives two quick claps. "See? Was that so hard?"

Loathing fills me until my skin feels ready to rupture.

Noah's right. I would die before working for him.

And I'd die before leaving Deke to Noah's mercies.

"On your feet now, Salton," Noah says cheerily. "Say goodbye to Eckhart. You'll get to talk to him for, oh, three minutes a day, work schedule permitting." He raises a hand and shouts over his shoulder. "Come in, boys."

"Get up slow," the woman—Miss Xi—says. We're right up against the Chinese border, and she has a BBC accent. "No sudden movements."

I don't want to do this.

I roll to my hands and knees, ignoring the chorus of protests from my back and ribs, pivoting just a little so my left side faces Xi. My heart throbs in my broken cheekbone and my night vision goggles bob ludicrously on my forehead. I pause to catch my breath, probably longer than I need, but she said "slow."

I move to stand, and instead groan. I painstakingly move my right hand to the outside of my thigh, as if to massage a pain.

Xi says, "You want to whimper, I'll get my whip."

I take a deep breath and slip my hand into my thigh pocket.

"One trick and I shoot you," Xi snaps.

I'm still facing the floor, on my knees and one hand.

The hand in my pocket pushes and holds a button.

My pocket beeps.

"Tell me, Noah," I say. "Are you familiar with the concept of a dead man switch?"

61

In the cabin doorway, Noah chortles. "Really, Salton? That's a tool of unintelligent madmen. I might question your sanity, but never your intelligence."

"Stay right where you are." The wooden floor hurts my knees; when did I get *those* bruises? "Just so there's no misunderstandings: I'm taking my hand out of my pocket."

My hand fits snugly into that thigh pocket.

Especially snugly, wrapped around my last brick of plastic explosive.

Very especially since I can't take my thumb off the detonator button. Even a moment's slip means death.

The greasy brick of plastique squirms beneath its wax paper wrapper, no matter how tightly I squeeze it.

With a methodical twist, I free my hand and hoist my prize high.

Noah's right. A dead man's switch is for unintelligent madmen.

I'd set the timer for three seconds. Long enough to push the button, release it, throw, and run. My thumb's over the timer, though. All anyone can see is the brick of explosive and my hand on the detonator.

Miss Xi—and her automatic pistol—remain focused on me, but she pulls in a deep breath. Even collapsed Deke stirs in his chair.

I straighten onto my knees. "I'm standing now."

Noah's eyes twitch uncertainly behind the beekeeper's veil. "You don't expect me to seriously believe you would destroy yourself."

"Wow." I shake my head. "You don't understand people at *all*, do you?"

"I understand people excellently. I made one of my fortunes off of people's desires."

My weapon beeps. "I love Deke *way* too much to leave him with you. Taking you with us? Shutting down your sick little research lab? That's gravy."

There's a faint metallic click from somewhere near the door.

I shake the greasy makeshift bomb. "Those people you called for? Tell them to move back."

Noah's weight shifts, just a hint.

"One step, and you die with us," I say. "You can't run out of blast radius before I let go. And I'm not dying alone."

Beep.

"Get back!" Noah shouts. He doesn't take his eyes off the bomb, as if willing my finger to remain on the button. He's still got too much confidence.

"You don't really see it, do you?" I say.

"Killing yourself has no future," Noah says. "I'm primarily concerned your hand will slip."

I lick my chapped lips. "Maybe I can't win—but I absolutely *refuse* to lose."

Noah's jaw drops a vital fraction of an inch.

He gets it now.

Curiosity flashes across the back of my brain. What had Noah done to build his empire? How many lives had he ruined even before he got to this malignant point?

What had a younger Noah done to not lose?

"We're leaving," I say.

"You step out of here and my boys will shoot you."

"I know. That's why you're coming with me."

"Unacceptable," Noah says.

"Would you rather die now?"

"Going with you has no future. You refuse to lose?" Noah's eyes narrow. Understanding my suicidal threat had shaken him, but now he found himself. "I also reject losing."

"You brought up negotiation," I say. "Ever hear of the win-win proposition?"

"Dreadful things."

"It's the only way out of here."

Deke says, "Nope."

I hadn't forgotten Deke—but he's not strong enough to get out of his chair.

But now the muzzle of my .38 semi-auto peeks over the arm of his wheelchair, pointing straight at Xi.

Deke is a wreck.

But he's doesn't look broken any more.

At Deke's voice, Xi takes her gun off me, swiveling towards Deke.

Deke fires.

Xi folds at the gut and stumbles backwards. There's no blood—is that stupid catsuit bulletproof?

Deke fires again.

A crimson fountain erupts from the top of Xi's head. She collapses against a pine wall, the blood texturing the varnish gleam.

I'm already moving, stumbling towards Xi, the detonator clenched in one fist.

Deke's turning the gun to Noah—but the fat bastard's already out the door, his cowardice propelling him faster than a rocket could.

Xi's pistol fell to the ground, and now lies near her twitching feet. I snatch it in my left hand.

Deke's got my .38 gripped in both hands, firing wildly through the open door into the darkness. He has this ferocious grin even as each shot bucks his wasted arms.

"The light!" I snap, dashing towards the door, stuffing Xi's pistol into a pocket.

I'm slamming the door even as Deke puts a bullet in the emergency light, dousing the cabin with the same darkness as the rest of Noah's compound.

I seize the back of Deke's collar and fling both of us to the ground.

The first AK-74 round punches through the front wall.

Deke gasps, "That woman right *needed* killing."

Another dozen rounds slice the air over our heads.

62

Hitting the floor *hurts*. My fractured ribs, my bruised back, my busted cheekbone, everything I'd injured seems to strike the varnished floorboards at once. My breath rushes out of me, and a haze of pain fogs my brain, drowning out even the barrage of AK-74 fire.

I do manage to keep my hand on the detonator.

It takes a moment before the pain clears and I can pull the night vision goggles down over my eyes. The cabin interior snaps into view in shades of green. The tables and the Wheel of Pain loom over us, sliced with the quickly-fading faint green bullet trails. Thunderous gunfire punches through the front wall, leaving bright green dots.

Deke lies beside me. Is he shot? No, he's moving his arm, getting himself ready to act despite being almost dead.

It's not that I really like tough men. But when you need toughness, nothing else suffices.

We can't stay here. If Noah's gunmen keep filling the building with bullets, eventually they'll nail us both.

I turn my head to the bomb in my hand. Without the cabin lights, the tiny readout on the detonator's clearly visible, blinking 03 over and over again.

Three seconds. Long enough to throw the explosive and run like hell. Except we're surrounded by walls. The snipers have blown the glass out of the windows, but the heavy drapes would catch anything.

Deke's wheelchair is on its side from where I hauled him out, one wheel turning. A bullet punctures its seat.

Another splits the air right over my head.

I take a deep breath. Clench my teeth. And roll onto my back.

The floor vibrates with gunfire.

Not much choice. I ignore the fear gibbering in the back of my brain and bring my hands together tight in front of my face so I can push two buttons.

The detonator beeps once more, then the 03 goes dark.

Glass shatters. Water splashes my face. The pitcher's gone.

The invisible band around my chest loosens just a touch, and I tuck the explosive back in its pocket.

Now to get out of here.

The cabin has no back door. If I open the front door, the shooters will cut me in half. But Deke's already pushing himself across the floor, staying as flat as possible, inching up to—

—the trap door.

Leading to a crawlspace.

I give a savage grin and scoot after him, keeping my limbs flat against the floor. Lying on my back, the easiest way to get there would be to shove with my legs, but each time I raised my knees from the ground I'd make myself a bigger target. I have to make do pulling with my arms and inching along with my feet, little shreds of traction.

Still, I beat Deke to the trap door. Find the notch of the handle. I have to raise my hand briefly to swing the door up, then I slither forward and drop out.

The crawlspace has a sick mugginess, the air thick and fervid. I don't want to imagine what might be buried down here that creates such fetid air. There's maybe two feet between the hard pebbly ground and the joists. I get my butt under me, lever myself to an elbow, and reach out the trap door to drag Deke the last couple feet into the slightly safer darkness.

The gunfire's quieter down here, and the infrared goggles show no bullet trails. There's a faint rectangle of coolness at the front of the crawlspace, maybe a foot across. I take a moment to breathe, straighten my legs, and collect myself.

There's blood in the back of my throat. Is my nose still bleeding? I pinch the bridge to try to stop it. My lips and chin are tacky and coppery.

"Tell me the plan," Deke says.

Find out how you could betray me. Put a bullet between your eyes. "The plan's long gone."

"Backup?"

"Blown."

"Shit."

"Yeah."

Deke looks even worse in the infrared goggles. His broken teeth are jagged spurs in his mouth. The infected gunshot wound in the side of his face burns white. And he stinks like a week-dead pig in an abandoned cheese factory.

He can stink all he wants, if he'll just stay alive.

"Did anyone else survive?" I ask.

Deke shakes his head. "Beck made it a few days. Gutshot, peritonitis."

His words drag me down a little further. If everyone else had somehow lived through the Newcastle raid, I would have dismantled Noah's whole complex to retrieve them.

I miss every one of them.

But, right now, the sad fact that my teammates are all dead simplifies our escape.

The gunfire slows, each shot growing further apart.

Silence.

That's the problem when your goons all have the same weapon, and they all start firing together. Their magazines all run dry simultaneously.

"Salton!" The shout is distant, and muffled by the walls and drapes, but I recognize Noah's voice.

I sit straight up under the trap door, exposing my head and shoulders. "You want to negotiate some more?" I shout back.

"Billie!" Deke hisses.

"Your death would be a shame," Noah shouts.

I'm sure his men are reloading right now, or swapping out half-exhausted magazines for fresh ones. I hop up, getting my butt on the cabin floor. "I hate to say it," I shout, "but you're right." I start crawling over towards the door. *Keep him talking.* "Everything being equal, everyone would rather live."

"My offer's still open," Noah shouts.

I hop to my feet. The refrigerator's a wreck. Chunks have been blown out of the torture wheel—good. Broken glass and spilled water and ruptured pill bottles mosaic the floor. "Sweeten the deal a little."

The AK-74's right near where I was standing when Noah shot me. I step towards it.

A single gunshot cracks through the front wall and splits the air inches from my shoulder.

I can't help flinching. But I still trot forward and snatch my own AK-74.

"You can talk with Deke more." Now that Deke and I are fish trapped in a barrel, Noah's being downright magnanimous. "As work permits. And you can spend time with him in between assignments. I had intended that to be a reward, but you can start with it. Just don't expect a raise later."

I dash back to the trap door and sit on the edge, stuffing the rifle into the crawlspace. "How about this? You take your generous offer, and stuff it up your—"

The barrage renews just as I slip back under the floor.

"Take the deal," Deke says. "We'll escape, first thing."

What, does he think I've gone soft? I hug the AK-74 stock to my chest. "Stay by the door."

"I can't lose you," Deke snarls. "Not again."

I stop. My heart's this madly twisting flutter. "You never will," I say. I lay the rifle down to cradle his maimed cheek in my hand. The infected wound feels like a knot of hot metal cupped in my palm.

Deke closes his eyes and leans into my touch.

Despite the bullets destroying everything above our heads, this very second is the most peaceful moment I've had since Newcastle.

For one precious breath, the world is whole.

Withdrawing my touch feels like ripping my hand off my body. "We get out of this together," I say. "Or we don't get out at all."

63

I'm a wreck of a human being.

Deke is in even worse shape.

But we don't have far to go. I can see a path to escape. All I need to do is clear a path out of this narrow, stinking crawlspace.

Dragging the AK-74 by the barrel, I scoot across clumpy clay and jagged pebbles until I get to the cabin's front wall.

The night vision goggles had revealed a cooler rectangle up here. My questing fingers found what I'd hoped for—an air vent. The crawlspace is noxious, but crawlspaces without ventilation can actually be toxic.

Flimsy aluminum clips hold the vent in place.

I scoot the rifle up next to me, lie on my left side to spare my ribs, and wait. Lying there, I can't help deliberately tensing and relaxing my back, trying to keep a little blood flow over that bruise. I can't take the time to stretch, even if I had the room, but I need to keep some flexibility despite the beating I've taken.

Deke needs me.

I listen to the gunfire like it's microwave popcorn. If I move too quickly, I'll only have half a batch. If I move too slow, I'm the one who will burn. But when the bullets slow down, I grab the vent clips in both hands, squeeze them together, and push the vent out of the hole to expose the night.

The infrared goggles highlight five men. Two of them are still shooting assault rifles at the cabin, aiming over my head. The other three are swapping magazines, somewhat clumsily. They haven't practiced enough to get the exchange down smooth, probably expecting that one thirty-round magazine would finish anyone.

They haven't practiced enough to survive.

I don't have time to waste by hurrying. Despite my pulse in my temples and the clenching in my gut, I painstakingly shift my own AK-74 into place and take aim.

Everything in me wants to take out the two active shooters first. But the fact that they're still shooting means that they're almost out of ammo. If the gunshots all stop at once, everyone will realize something's wrong. I need to take out the three men who are replacing their magazines with full ones.

The man at the end of the line raises his replenished rifle to his shoulder.

I plant two rounds between his eyes.

The gunshots are deafening in the enclosed crawlspace. There's a pair of earplugs in my pocket, but too late now—my ears start that annoying ringing that shouts *I'm an idiot.*

But outside, they'll sound just like two more shots amidst the barrage.

The goon in the middle raises his rifle.

One of my shots misses, but the other takes his throat and puts him down.

But one of the active shooters shifts. The brick wall beside me lets out this cracking noise. Shattered concrete flashes past my vision.

He's seen me.

I can't tell if he's told the others, what with the high-pitched whine in my ears, but I put two bullets in him anyway.

More bullets strike the edge of my shelter.

Yep, he said something.

But I only have to move my rifle a fraction of a degree to change targets, and I have nice steady brick to balance the rifle against.

Bam-bam.

Bam-bam.

Five more corpses, cooling in the Myanmar night.

As far as I can tell, the night is silent. Which pretty much means nobody's shooting any more. I can't hear anything quieter than a rifle.

Noah's a coward. With his thugs dead, he's running for… probably, more thugs.

I scoot back to Deke. "You hear anything?"

He slides his hands from his ears and shakes his head. His lips are moving, but my stunned ears can't hear anything.

If I never hear another human voice, *I can't lose you, not again* aren't bad last words to hear. There's better, but those aren't bad.

Then we're up out of the crawlspace. The cabin looks like a fourth-hand colander that even the thrift store would reject. Deke can't move under his own strength, so I drag him up. I right the battered wheelchair. The seat and back are full of holes, but the wheels still turn and it seems solid enough.

We get Deke in the chair. He's given up asking questions, but lets me knot the woven plastic seat belt around him.

I put my heavy steel .38 semi-auto and Xi's silver .32 automatic in his lap.

Deke clenches one in each hand.

Then we charge into the night.

64

With each turn of the wheelchair's hard rubber tires, a vibration travels up the frame through the plastic grips and into my hands. An annoying silent grind, or a pronounced squeak? The droning two-tone whine in my stunned ears smothers any hope of me hearing either. I just have to hope that any noise doesn't attract attention.

Not that pushing a wheelchair through a war zone isn't going to attract attention.

Flames shroud all eight of the compound's guard towers, lofting clouds of whitish-gray bitter smoke across the slanted grassy ground and up into the cavernous night sky. The bombed-out security center up the hill is a seething red pit vomiting noxious black haze, the dead generators a merrily crackling brightness across from them. While Noah's goons were filling Deke's cottage with bullets, floating cinders re-ignited the barracks roof and transformed it to a plain of flame gnawing at the walls beneath.

The good news is, with all these flames, nobody can be using those cheap-ass night vision goggles Noah stocks. Those pricey assault rifles won't do any good if the goons can't see us.

I can't use the knock-off goggles Rob got me either, but I don't need night vision. The ribbon of concrete walkway leading to the docks gleams amber in the distant firelight, slashes of shadows marking off the powerless light poles. And anything that moves is an enemy.

"Deke." My nose is full of blood and my ears filled with that warbling drone, so I have no idea how loud I'm talking. "I still can't hear. Thump the arm of the chair twice if I need to stop. Or shoot whatever it is and I'll keep going."

A single impact vibrates the wheelchair grip.

Rib fractured. Bradley's tape job bought me some time, but each breath is an aching stab that promises full-on agony, and soon. My back's a spiderweb of aches and probably some bruises that go all the way through to my abs. Busted cheekbone: bonus! The AK-74 bounces off my left shoulder and thwaps my butt with every step, but I'm not dropping it.

I'm *so* done with the Catwoman impression. We're moving up to the Punisher.

Maybe full-on Rorschach if we don't get out of here *now*.

But the dock is right there, a line of aluminum panels bobbing on plastic floats, sticking thirty feet or so into the water. The river itself must be fifty yards wide, a dark susurrus with rippling reflections flickering across the fast-flowing current. I can't even guess how deep the water goes or what's beneath it.

And not just a boat, but a few boats, illuminated by the flaming guard tower still standing a few yards upstream. A huge flat barge that looks able to carry half a dozen compact cars dominates one side of the floating dock, reflected fires rippling across its shallow metal hull as it rolls with the river's flow. On the other side of the dock: two twelve-foot aluminum dinghies, each lumbered with a massive outboard motor.

They're absolutely beautiful.

Pissed Off Widow had called using the boats stupid, but I didn't see many choices. She'd taken the road, which meant a bunch of Noah's thugs were right behind her. I could imagine all sorts of things on that road right now, and we were in no shape to fight our way through any of them.

I boldly wheel right out onto the bobbing dock and jerk to a halt by the closest dinghy. Deke is already struggling to shift forward and climb out, but he doesn't have the strength to lift himself. I stomp the wheel lock and grab Deke.

He's not heavy. But when I hoist Deke, the stab in my side and the shudder in my spine bleeds my strength. I hear him gasp, even through the ringing in my ears—they must be recovering. "I got you," I wheeze, and guide his faltering steps so he can slip straight down into the middle of the dinghy. He sprawls on the ribbed aluminum deck, hands feebly clutching at the rear bench seat as he tries to brace himself against the gunwale. One of the shipped oars comes loose from its bracket, clattering to the deck.

The ache to grab Deke's hand is stronger than the throbbing bruise covering my back. Instead, I dump my backpack beside him, place the AK-74 stock-down next to that, and hop in.

Dammit, I should have made sure the boat *started* before putting Deke in! I'll never get him out of the boat by myself, not now. I'm too exhausted to heave him up to the dock, too exhausted to think. That's why you have plans, detailed plans, so when your brain overloads on fear and adrenaline and cortisol you can follow the plan and come out the other side. Rob's not wrong, calling it a script.

Heart pounding in my throat, I hop down.

A kick tells me the tank is full.

I yank the pull cord, and the outboard starts right up.

Relief floods me. Deke won't pay (again) for my blithering incompetence, my lack of trust, all my mistakes.

I clamber past Deke to the bow. The dinghy wobbles like it's going to tip. The bottom's broad enough that it should be okay, but with our luck I'm not risking it. Two quick twirls of rope, and the bow's free. I climb back to the stern, careful not to lean on Deke as I pass him, and start unlashing the second line.

Up the sloping hillside of Noah's compound, the night is ablaze. I glimpse hazy silhouettes in front of the fires, dashing back and forth.

Some of those figures are running towards us.

I bet they've heard the boat.

One of those shifting silhouettes is a lot rounder than the others. It's got to be Noah. But he's extra blocky—body armor?

And is that shadow in his hand a knife?

One day I'll take Noah's knife away. Teach him not to play with sharp objects.

With the stern line unlashed all but a single loop around the mooring point, I pause. With the line straining around my left hand, I weasel the last block of plastique out of my thigh pocket with my right. I only need one hand to crank the timer up to thirty seconds, push the button, and give it a gentle underhand toss.

My recovering ears catch the high notes of the bomb's clattering impact against the second dinghy's deck.

My ears also catch the sound of gunfire.

I whip the last loop off the dock and rev the motor.

From what I remember of the map, upstream leads to China. Beneath the flickering torch of the flaming guard tower, I aim the dinghy downstream, near the middle of the river, and gun the motor.

We're out of blast range when my last explosive turns the night to light. I reflexively hunch my shoulders, as if I could pull them over my ears, but the noise doesn't seem to make the ringing any worse. I glance back over the snarling motor to see bits of dock, barge, dinghy, and probably puree of thug spattering down into the racing water. A couple figures stumble backwards, hands upraised to shield themselves from the debris.

Then we're around the first bend, cloaked by the thick veils of overgrown trees. The horrific stinks of burning wood, melting plastic, and scorched metal hang heavy on my tongue as the utter darkness of the Burmese jungle engulfs the river, the dinghy, Deke, and me.

65

The bugs churning the darkness are appalling. I have to pull my mask back up over my mouth just to keep from choking. The soft microfiber stings my bludgeoned, nearly-broken nose.

Noah's flaming compound is a brightness in the sky behind us, but the light doesn't do anything to illuminate the river. I'm forced to fall back to Rob's third-rate night vision goggles, which aren't great for this kind of work. The riverbanks are only a little brighter than the water, and the drooping overgrown trees are nearly invisible shawls that trail down over us. The water glitters in infrared, tiny variations as the river skips over submerged logs and stones and who knows what.

Straddling the rear bench seat, with one hand on the outboard motor's tiller, I'm forced to slow to only a few miles an hour. The ringing in my ears has softened, but I still can't hear the swarms of bugs battering themselves senseless against the exposed skin of my ears.

At least my nose has stopped bleeding. Bloody drying mucus still clogs my sinuses, though, making my head feel stuffed with cotton. As the river carries us further from the pyre of Noah's compound, I eventually hit a straight stretch where I feel safe enough to take a deep breath, lean over the stern, pull down the face mask, and blow my nostrils clear of clotted blood one at a time. My busted cheekbone snarls with each blast. The goggles show bright green knots of Beaks-scum splashing into the water and vanishing.

I pull the mask up and finally get to inhale through my nose. My sinuses burn with rich humid fecund jungle air, the smells of trees and brush and every kind of plant, growing for centuries without the purges of cold or snow.

Heavenly.

Then my attention's back on the river. I have no chance of noticing submerged rocks with the goggles—everything's in shades of green. The water sparkles the most green in the middle, though. I think that's the fastest-flowing part, so I try to keep in the sparkle. The banks are far enough away that I couldn't hit them with a thrown rock, even if I was healthy.

The sturdy aluminum dinghy's nose is an upraised triangle against the river. With all the weight near the rear, the dinghy moves easily. I could easily crank the throttle up above a quarter, but a nighttime charge down an unfamiliar jungle river is a great way to drown.

There's a weird triangle in the water's brightness up ahead, like the heat is dividing around something. I veer the boat to the side and peer over into the water as we pass it. The night vision goggles vaguely suggest a darker green shape below the water. A submerged rock?

This trip is going to be like one of those old racing games. But if I hit a banana peel, the whole boat will flip. Piranha are Amazonian, but what lives in Myanmar rivers? Crocodiles? Some species of skeletonizing fish that *hasn't* seized the popular imagination? Or just really horrible infectious diseases?

I still ache—no, now that nobody's chasing us, I downright *hurt*. My fractured ribs promise weeks of suffering, and awful bruises radiate out from the small of my back. My hands are scraped and scabby, my clothes are filthy, and beneath those clothes I'm still wearing cave mud sauced with Pissed Off Widow pee. I haven't slept properly in I don't know how long, and exhaustion has sifted through every fiber of every muscle and drained into my very bones.

Worse, I really don't know where we are. Up near the Chinese border, sure. But in these mountains, we could pass within a quarter of a mile of a village and not catch a hint of it. I've got a canteen with maybe a cup of water in it, and I think there's a protein bar in the bottom of my bag, under all the backup tapes. And we're stuck on the river, because I'm in no shape to hack a path through the jungle, even if I had an idea where we are or where we're going. This stretch of jungle should be called *1001 Ghastly Tropical Diseases Just For You!* We're so far out of the Tourist Triangle, if the military finds us they'll just shoot us and throw our bodies in the river.

But Deke is at my feet.

He's slumped against the gunwale, head tipped back, one elbow resting on the aluminum trim like it's a car window. I can't quite hear if he's snoring or not, my ears aren't that recovered. The goggles offer new insights into his wounds—the infections burn hot. His cheek has a bright spot right under the nasty stitches, tendrils radiating out through his jaw and up into his brow. From the way the side of his cheek glows, I'm betting he's got some dental abscesses from his poor broken teeth. His white cotton shirt and pants hide the wounds on his arms and legs, but his swollen bare feet glow bright.

My overflowing heart hurts more than my fractured ribs. My poor, poor baby.

And I'd left him there.

I'd believed he'd turned.

I can't stand myself right now.

Deke stirs. He turns his head so that his working eye can fix on me. The hand that isn't draped over the gunwale fumbles back to find my shin, right above my boot. His gentle squeeze makes my heart quicken even more than navigating an uncharted Myanmar river in the dark.

I can almost hear his whispered words. Instead, I have to shake my head. "I'm sorry, my ears are still buzzing."

"I missed you." He's not shouting.

He's sitting at my feet, and I burn to collapse at his. "Deke. Bear—" No. I don't get to call him that.

I don't deserve to.

The river is turning. I tap the tiller a few degrees.

Deke squeezes my shin, not strong. Just enough to let me know he's there.

I treasure his touch.

In a few more minutes, I might never get it again.

The prow settles back into the brighter green of the river's curve. "Deke. I have to tell you."

He waits for a beat. "What is it?" Deke can tell I'm having trouble speaking. His tone is encouraging without pushing.

If he decides to push me overboard, I'll let him.

"When we hit Noah." My face is burning in the dark. "Back in Portugal. His email…" My stomach is a pit of acid.

I have to spit the words. "He said you'd turned."

Deke's hand on my shin remains still.

I have to finish it. I have to admit it. "I didn't come here to break you out."

Deke says nothing.

I can hear a few insects now, buzzing above the motor's low rumble and the sluicing of water against the keel.

The silence stretches unbearably.

"Let me get this straight," Deke finally drawls. "You mean, you're saying, that you broke into Noah's compound. Alone. You blew everything to hell."

"Not everything," I say feebly. "And I had Rob and Bradley for the first bit."

Deke shakes his head slowly. "I don't know what that hellhole looked like when you showed up, but I don't rightly think that two bricks were standing on top of each other when we left. And who knows how many people you killed. Just—and let me be sure I've got this right here—just so you could come in and wallop my ass personal-like."

My face burns hot beneath my mask. "Yeah. I bought the story. Bought the whole thing."

"All right then." Deke's quiet for a breath. "In that case, Noah ought to be glad that you didn't show up to rescue me. You mighta done some damage."

Sudden anger flashes through my gut. "I'm serious, Deke! I left you there! I blew it! I thought you were dead, I thought you'd turned, I didn't trust you and you deserve—you deserve better."

Don't make a joke of this, don't you dare *blow me off!*

With an effort, Deke raises his head to look square at my face. He hauls his hand up to cup my knee. "Billie," he says. "Babe Billie. The important thing is, you came for me. You wouldn'ta done blown up half a mountain and a whole James Bond villain lair 'less you really loved me."

The twisty river is treacherous, but I drop the throttle to where the motor's barely above an idle.

Bending over makes my ribs stab worse and my back scream.

I don't care.

I don't remember putting my arm around his shoulders, or the other arm, but he's in there, his strength whittled down to gaunt bones but so wonderfully alive, his untouched cheek pressed warm into my neck, my night vision goggles clunking against his scalp, with the tears running down my face and the tremble in my back swelling towards a detonation of full-on bawling. Deke's shaking too, all the encysted fear and pain of his last two weeks ready to explode in my arms.

I'm not all right.

Deke certainly isn't all right.

But *we* are all right. It'll take time, but we are going to be fine, eventually.

I want to ask him to forgive me.

But with the outboard turned way low, and with my ears recovering, I can hear another motor.

A *big* motor.

Running full-out, howling at its limit.

Coming up behind us.

66

Forgiveness and acceptance can wait.

Escape can't.

Deke tenses in my arms—he hears the roaring pursuit too.

The Myanmar jungle night no longer feels peaceful. The massive trees, trailing overgrown fingerling branches into the shallows at either side of the river, loom like brick walls, impenetrable and burned-out and broken as Deke and I are. The sky is a dark empty vault overhead, pitiless stars burning pinpricks in the night vision goggles. Even the river is flowing more quickly, like it's caught our urgency.

I'd blown up one dock. Taken out the boats.

But now, my exhaustion-fogged brain reminds me that the security system showed two docks.

Forget the IQ tests, the degrees, the research paper my prof was willing to kill me to steal: I'm an idiot.

The night vision goggles only hint at the river's character. The fastest-flowing part is a brighter green. I've had us puttering down the river, keeping to the middle, trying to avoid the little green-on-green triangles and lines that seem to indicate submerged rocks and sunken logs and probably crocodiles or invasive piranha or whatever who-knows-what lives in Burmese rivers?

But the howling motor behind us is getting closer.

And we only have one way we can go.

If everything looks like a video game, it's time to kick it up to expert level and get out of here.

"Hang on!" I sit straight and twist the throttle.

The dinghy shoots down the middle of the river like I've stuffed an angry rhino under it.

The countless bugs feel like a bitter snowstorm, tiny hard shells that whizz past me. Some pock on my cheeks. One little insect slips into a nostril, so I snort and yank the microfiber face mask back up. My heart thuds against my aching ribs and bruised back.

Deke moves clumsily to grab the gunwale and brace himself against my legs. After two weeks of imprisonment and illness and our sudden mad dash, he's at the end of his endurance.

"Deke!" I shout over the snarling outboard.

He looks up, the night vision goggles rendering his injuries in mottled shades of green.

"Earpiece in the bag," I shout. "See if you can pick anything up." He can't adjust the earpiece very well without the smartphone app, but he can do a rough frequency walk. "Get me some intel on what's ahead, or chatter from Noah's thugs."

Deke nods. Having a task makes his hands more certain as he goes straight to the lower right outside pocket on my bag. Not only do I put every piece of gear in the same place every time, I made sure Deke knew how I packed. And I knew where Deke kept his brass knuckles and radio beacons and traction pads and all his other toys. He finds the receiver right off and stuffs it in his ear, then clips the mic around his throat. He always joked that my throat mic would strangle him, but tonight it hangs loosely and he has to cinch it up a couple inches.

My own throat tightens.

Triple triangles! I'd glanced away from the river, and the subtle hints of danger appeared in that second. I swerve the boat between the unseen obstructions, wrenching the tiller from side to side and back. The keel scrapes something at the last one, knocking us aside, but we don't tip and half a second later we're straight down the middle again.

The river is getting rougher, the submerged obstacles thicker and thicker.

I don't dare look away again.

My bruised back itches. I want to glance behind us, to see if our pursuers have come into view. My ears still have a bit of a droning ring in them from blowing up the dock, so I can't even tell if there's another motor snarling back there.

At the edge of my vision, Deke sits up straight.

"What is it?" I shout.

He's talking, but not to me. The goggles show his face getting brighter.

I yank the tiller to get us around some wide flat disturbance in the glowing green water. I must *focus* through my exhaustion and swirling passion, or we both die.

Deke looks up at me and says something.

"Can't hear you!" I shout. The outboard is thunder in my ears.

Deke fills his wasted chest and shouts:

"Waterfall! Big-ass waterfall!"

67

It wasn't my imagination. The river is getting rougher, the submerged debris more common.

Because somewhere up ahead, the water gets really shallow and plunges off a cliff.

Night vision only shows a few hundred yards of water ahead before a rightward turn around a rocky outcropping and densely knotted foliage. Is that really a turn, or is that the end?

"How far?" I shout.

"'Bout a quarter mile," Deke shouts back.

At our speed, that's nothing. I drop the motor back to an idle and scan the riverbanks. Thick trees majestically draped in moss and vines, limned in black and synthetic green, cage us in.

The river *is* flowing more quickly.

I want to interrogate Deke, find out who he's talking to, but there's no time.

Noah's men will have night vision goggles a little crappier than mine. They know the river, though. They probably have maps, and depth finders, and a native guide who's explored this terrain every day of his twenty years and who thinks he's gone to heaven if you give him a can of Coke.

I still have a bunch of my breaking and entering tools, but they're mostly useless now. I have an AK-74M with three thirty-round magazines. No explosives, no grenades, no nothing. Deke has my .38 semi-auto and Psycho Bitch Xi's silver .32 automatic. Plus, he's wearing white cotton. In the jungle. At night. I might as well spray-paint a glow-in-the-dark SHOOT ME on his chest.

There's no time for negativity. But how do I fight and win?

Glancing over my shoulder, the river behind us is clear for a couple hundred yards then veers out of view. The river's curve hides our pursuers, but their motor's roaring smothers our outboard's grumble. Sound carries a ways over water, but Noah's goons can't be more than a couple minutes behind us.

Simple is best. I turn the tiller to the side and rev the motor. The water's moving even more swiftly now, dragging us towards the unseen falls, so I have to turn the tiller further to get us to the shore right where I want. I even have to goose the outboard into high for a moment to go straight upstream until the prow bumps my target.

One of the massive trees lining the riverbank fell into the water, maybe only a few months ago. The trunk is about five feet thick, leafy branches still poking out of the side exposed to air. It won't live much longer—the water will eat it away—but for now, it's shelter.

When the dinghy bumps thick corrugated bark I loop the stern line around a convenient branch, lashing the line against itself so that a hard yank will slip us loose. The water tugs at the aluminum frame, but the boat quickly settles into place, nose bobbing downstream. The trunk sits about a yard out of the water, high enough to provide some shelter but low enough that I have to crouch to use it.

The boat ends up with its nose pointing downstream, stabilized by the current. It's not even vaguely an ideal place, but it's as good as we're going to get.

When I cut the outboard, the night fills with the constant buzzing of insects and the approaching snarl of another motor. The insects instantly converge, mindlessly battering themselves against my face mask and exposed forehead.

"We're stopped," Deke says.

"We hole up here," I say. I grab the AK-74 and lay the barrel across the tree trunk, pointing upstream. The bobbing dinghy makes this a worse sniper's nest than it is a hiding place, but I'll have to make it work.

Maybe a few dozen carefully targeted rounds will dissuade our pursuers.

If not, I tug the line and send us on our way. I don't know how big this waterfall is, but a thousand-yard plunge with an aluminum dinghy parachute offers us better odds than Noah.

Pissed Off Widow had said that the river was stupid.

Guess she was right.

I kneel on the cramped deck behind the rear bench seat. My knees protest the metal deck, and the constant small shifts as the dinghy rocks with the current makes it impossible to find a comfortable posture. I shift the AK-74 across the fallen tree's trunk, searching for a good place to brace the assault rifle. The aroma of crushed green moss fills my nose and my hands quickly grow slick, but I find a convenient notch right where a branch splits away from the trunk, elbow planted in a notch where another branch splits out.

The dinghy's bobbing makes steady aim almost impossible. I keep my finger on the trigger guard, despite the urge to be ready to fill our pursuers with steel-jacketed rounds the moment they appear. My heart is a runaway train car. I have to concentrate to not hyperventilate. I have to wait until they're close enough for me not to miss.

Either I shoot every one of our pursuers dead, or Deke and I die.

Either way, this would be over soon.

I lick my lips. "Deke," I say. "You know I love you, don't you?"

Deke's trembling hand touches my shoulder. "I'd blow up a mountain for you, too." His fingers tighten for a moment, then fall away. My bear doesn't have the strength to hold his arm up. I ache to take his hand, but instead I've got the AK-74's clammy plastic stock and metal trigger mechanism.

The tree groans and creaks when I lean on it. The top looks fine, but the water must have eaten it away below.

I exhale deeply, trying to calm my heart. I'm about to ask Deke who he had on the radio, but there's a sudden surge upstream, and our pursuers rush into view.

The boat isn't lit, but its warmth makes it burn in the night vision goggles. This isn't a dinghy or a barge—it's a full-on a yacht. A man stands at the prow, hands to his head. There's a green-limned cabin just behind him, with a pilot's station up on the roof and a long, low deck behind. The deck is jammed with people.

Maybe it's not Noah's thugs? Could there be innocent bystanders out here?

While weapons don't stand out well on night vision goggles, I do see cut-out shadows of AK-74s on people's shoulders and held across chests.

It's Noah's goons.

The good news is, with that many people crowded that close together, I'm sure to hit someone.

But I'm not sure I've brought enough bullets for everyone.

I bring my cheek to the AK-74 and line up the sights. The barrel wobbles with each twitch of the river. I can't get a clear, steady shot.

I gotta wait. Let them get closer.

Hope they don't see the muzzle flash.

Hope my rotting tree holds together long enough for me to finish them.

Hope they don't have a rocket launcher, or grenade launcher, or brick of plastic explosive and a reckless disregard for their own safety.

I hold myself still, hoping that they can't pick out my head and shoulders above the tree. Maybe they'll see my body heat, but think I'm an endangered clouded leopard or something. The air feels even muggier than before. Dampness glues my microfiber face mask to my face.

The yacht slows.

I bring the sights to bear on the man on the prow. The dinghy bobs beneath me, making my aim wobble. I tense a little, trying to compensate, but that only makes things worse.

The point man's a bad target anyway. Everybody'll be looking forward. Now that the yacht's coming straight at us I see only a narrow slice of the men in the back, though. That'll be a hard shot, but maybe they'll think I'm sniping from the riverbank.

No, there's a better target. One lone man. The most difficult target of all, but the most valuable.

I make myself breathe and relax.

Wait.

Watching the boat bobble in the rifle sights.

"Hold 'em long as you can," Deke whispers. "You got this."

I want to turn to Deke.

Instead, I let my finger slip from the guard and squeeze the trigger.

One shot. It takes me by surprise—it always does, that keeps me from flinching. At least we're in open air here, it won't damage my hearing so badly.

I miss.

The yacht slows, the motor's roar dropping to a giant's snore. Did they hear me shoot?

Willing the dinghy to still beneath me, I line up another shot and fire.

I hit!

The pilot on the yacht's roof staggers back, toppling out of sight.

There's a stir of motion in the back of the yacht. The figure in the prow starts dancing and waving his arms.

I shift the rifle to aim into the churning mass of goons and start shooting. Single shots, each carefully aimed, trying to ride with the dinghy's bobble rather than fighting it. Aim over their heads, pull the trigger as the dinghy rises and shifts my aim down.

The screams say it works.

A few yards to our side, the world comes apart in a crash of lightning.

68

The river sprays up in a thunderous fountain, spraying mud and muck over Deke and I. The blast rattles my teeth and knocks my aim completely astray. The dinghy slews wildly against the tree trunk we're anchored to. If I wasn't kneeling sore-kneed against the aluminum deck, I would have been knocked into the water. I feel Deke tumble to his side.

The men on Noah's yacht launched a grenade at us.

The yacht is still trolling towards us, drawn more by the waterfall's current than the idling motor. Nobody's taken the downed pilot's position, and the yacht's veering towards the far bank, exposing its flank.

And its passengers.

Too many glowing green targets to count. Their grenade launcher should stand out, glowing with heat, but I don't see it. I prop myself against the tree again, take aim, and start pulling the trigger. Each round sends a stabbing pain through my fractured ribs, but the tree absorbs the worst of force. The AK-74 will go through a whole magazine in seconds, but I make myself target each shot.

Men fall.

Then the tree sends new vibrations up into my elbows. Bullets hiss past my ears.

They've seen my muzzle flash.

I sight the yacht's slightly less crowded deck for one more shot, and glimpse the stubby hot shape of a recently used grenade launcher being hoisted in someone's arms.

"Crap," I say.

"Now would be good," Deke shouts. "Or now? I like now!"

Before I can shoot again, my hand finds the rope lashing us to the tree and yanks, hard.

The knot dissolves.

The dinghy starts downstream again, pushed by the current.

I pull the rifle back in and try to double over behind the stern.

We're a few yards away when thunder roars again, raining mud and bits of wood down on us.

Our shelter is gone.

We're adrift towards the waterfall.

Trapped.

I seize the AK-74, ignoring the pain in my flank and my back and my knees and everywhere else. Maybe we can't escape. Even if we defeated all of Noah's men, we'd probably die of those ghastly tropical diseases anyway.

But if I'm a dead woman, I'm taking a huge honor guard to Hell with me.

I bring the AK-74 to my shoulder, sight, and fire.

The impact is like getting stabbed in the lung.

Doesn't matter. I won't need the lungs much longer anyway.

More bullets whizz past my ear.

The night vision goggles show someone hoisting the grenade launcher again. Freshly reloaded, ready to shoot again.

I shoot. Another thug falls. Not the one with the grenade launcher.

"I love you, Deke!" I scream, pulling the trigger again.

There's another burst of lightning—no, not a burst.

A streak of angry fire.

From the sky.

It plunges into the yacht.

A new sun detonates on the water.

The light ruptures my night vision goggles, filling my eyes with pain. I slam my eyes shut, but the glare burns purple through the squinched lids. Shaken by the ongoing roar of the explosion, I crumple back, dropping the assault rifle on the deck and clawing the goggles off my head.

Dropping the goggles feels like losing the bowling ball anchored to my forehead. The nasty humid air is a relief around my eye sockets and around the back of my head.

My abused ears are ringing again, not as bad as with the plastic explosive, but bad enough to flatten the sounds of screaming men and Deke's raucous laughter.

The yacht is a floating puddle of flame, burning brightly enough to transform the trees along the riverbanks into flickering macabre columns and cryptic tangles of shadow. I see glimpses of men splashing around the wreckage. I inhale the toxic stink of burning plastic.

"What?" I say.

Deke tugs my shirt. He's holding out my earpiece.

I take it.

"Go," Deke says into his throat mic.

"Don't you *ever* throw a party without inviting me," Bradley says. "You bitch."

69

The air isn't merely humid, it's soaking wet with spray so thick that the bugs have given up and gone home. The quickening current hauls our unpowered dinghy pell-mell.

I yank the outboard's starter. My ribs shriek again, but the motor fires right up.

By the time I get the dinghy's nose pointed upstream, the guttering flames of Noah's yacht expose the waterfall.

The riverbed drops a yard amidst rounded crags and spars of exposed bedrock, tumbling towards another drop. Beyond those short rapids, the ground ends in an irregular curve. The sky beyond is picking up faint haze of pink from the approaching sunrise. Even through the waterfall's mist, I can see that beyond the waterfall is a whole lot of absolutely nothing.

"We have a winch," Bradley says in my ear. "Stay on the river if you can, we'll pull you up."

"Easy for you to say," I grumble. I have the outboard motor cranked all the way up, but it's not powerful enough to overcome the current.

The dinghy's oozing downstream.

All I can do is control where we hit.

Water splashes irregularly. It's one of Noah's goons, struggling to keep his head above the water as passes us on the race to oblivion.

Half a second later, he hits a spur of rock.

I don't see him again.

I force my attention back to steering the dinghy. Behind me, Deke is on his knees, gripping the forward bench seat. The gunwale's easier to hold, but when we hit a rock he'd lose his fingers.

And we are definitely going to hit a rock.

The dinghy hits something under the water and bounces aside. I curse and wrench the tiller, knocking us further off-course. The current's dragging us backwards, so the outboard's effects are reversed. I pull it back, just barely getting us within a couple feet of a massive irregular stone standing at the head of the first rapids.

With my other hand, I loop the stern rope around a spur of rock.

The dinghy wrenches and swings. The side clangs against the rock. The whole boat tips, making my heart rattle my ribs and my teeth clench—

—but the line holds.

The rope grinds against the stone, and the dinghy creaks and screeches where its flank batters the rock, but we're anchored in place.

Deke laughs with honest mirth. They joy of being alive, of being free.

I can't help joining in.

"You all right?" Bradley says in my ear.

I get Deke's attention and tap my throat. He nods, disconnects the throat mic, and hands it to me. I have to expand it by a couple inches to cinch it around my neck.

"We are okay."

"That's you right by the waterfall? Tied up to a rock?"

"Yep."

"Two minutes," Bradley says. "And next time you go renegade on us, keep your damn earpiece in. We thought that was you remaking Road Warrior. Blew a couple carloads of Noah's troopers to shit before we figured out they were chasing some crazy Chinese chick and a bunch of sick people."

There's a sudden knot in my gut. "Did they make it out?"

"The Chinese chick? Once we blew up the assholes chasing her, yeah."

So Pissed Off Widow and Noah's victims got away. The knot in my gut moves up into my throat.

Don't get me wrong, I'm not inviting Pissed Off Widow to any parties or anything, but I'm glad she escaped.

There's a burst of noise from the burning ruin of Noah's yacht, as the fire hits something. Flame puffs in a lambent cloud, and a chunk the size of a kitchen chair goes flying into the night. Galley propane tank, maybe?

Next to us, aluminum grinds on stone.

Our taut anchor line rubs against the stone, clearing algae to expose bare ragged stone.

"I don't know if this is going to hold," I shout to Deke above the tumult. "Can you get on the rock?"

"Right now, I can go anywhere!" Deke shouts. He's grinning. That horrible wound in the side of his face glistens in the distant firelight. I think he's cracked it open.

I make sure my little backpack is still in the dinghy, containing the backup tapes documenting Noah's work. A portable museum of horrors.

I've just started ruining "Sir" Jack Noah.

The rock is slippery and slimy, but there's a big enough flat patch for Deke to sprawl on, and a ledge for me to sit on a couple feet past that. Deke's saved up some strength during our boat ride: with his help, heaving him up only half-kills my ribs and back. I set the backpack in his lap, hand him the two handguns, then set the AK-74 next to him.

Who knows what kind of winch Bradley's got? I grab the spare coil of rope from the floor and drag myself up onto the rock. The dinghy bobs more easily without our weight in it, and the rope now looks strong enough to support it forever. Go figure.

I settle down on the clammy shelf of rock, instantly drenching my butt with sodden algae. I can feel the dirt beneath my clothes soaking it in, resurrecting the cavern mud. Was that only earlier tonight? Sitting in the Burmese night, the mist just barely tinted with pre-dawn pinkness and the burning yacht, it feels like a distant college memory.

Deke is lying on his side, both arms resting on a shelf of rock. His white cotton outfit has already sponged up mud and dirt and algae, but his face has a relaxation I haven't seen since before Newcastle.

A sudden light gleams overhead, spotlighting us.

I wince, glancing upriver, putting my hand on the AK-74.

Nobody shoots.

Now that I'm listening, I can hear the chopper's engine. It's a different roar than the waterfall, two titanic sounds struggling for dominance.

"The waterfall makes the air choppy," Bradley says in my earpiece. "We'll have to haul you up about forty feet."

"Deke first," I say.

"It's your party, you throw out whoever you want."

"Damn straight."

In another moment, a simple chest-and-groin harness comes down, dangling on the end of a heavy nylon rope. Deke tries to argue, sending me up first, but he's not strong enough to fight me off.

It's easy to ignore the sharp pain of my ribs as I fasten the last buckles around his chest. I don't have to last much longer.

Deke's lips taste of blood and sickness and hope.

His hand touches my cheek.

Then I step back and say "Clear."

I can't hear Deke's parting shout as he's cranked up into the sky, dangling his feet and the bag of backup tapes. But he's said *I love you* often enough that I can read the words on his lips.

He's barely gone for ten seconds when I hear another voice, down closer to the water.

Enough light splashes down from the helicopter's spotlight for me to see a face, surrounded in orange, hugging the lee of the rock, struggling to keep a grip.

It's Noah.

70

Shock blocks my breath.

Perched on this slippery chunk of stone, right over a waterfall, about to escape the jungle and Burma and a thousand deaths, breathing in this fog of mist and algae tinted with smoke, I didn't expect to see Noah's pale face bobbing fractions of an inch above the tumultuous current.

The only thing sustaining him is the bright orange life preserver, a heavy foam tube strapped to his chest and around the back of his neck. It's scorched, as is his hair. Blisters mark the back of his right hand as it scrabbles at the slick rock.

My hand snatches for the handguns. Deke must have taken the silver automatic I took from Xi's cooling corpse—can't blame him for that, we'll steal a mansion so we can get the damned thing framed and hang it above the fireplace. But the .38's still right where I put it, and the plastic grip fits nicely in my hand.

Noah's right in the front sight. I don't remember aiming.

My finger is on the trigger.

I've never shot a helpless person before.

Especially not in the face.

But there's a first time for everything.

Noah shouts, loud as he can but barely audible above the waterfall and the helicopter. "Forty million!" His voice is a high-pitched screech.

The .38 wavers.

I don't care about the money.

But truly, I've never killed a helpless person.

I've killed many people, yeah. But they all had weapons. They all tried to kill me. When I'd set the remote-control gun turrets at the compound against the guards, those guards had been carrying rifles. They would have killed me.

But that's a whole different thing from seeing someone's helpless face, trapped in a voracious current, and putting a round between their eyes.

But it's fucking Jack Noah.

This man killed my friends. Co-workers.

He used us. Set Rob up to kill me.

Tortured Deke.

Used what he learned to murder *how* many freelancers?

He made me believe Deke had turned.

Made me believe that love didn't own the human heart.

"Fifty million!" Noah shouts. "Bearer bonds! And I forget you and yours! Just help me!"

Fuck the money.

And fuck Noah. He's not important.

The important question is, am I a murderer?

71

Even using a spur of rock as a pulley for the rope, hauling Noah from the river ignites my every pain. My ribs, my back, the bruises and scrapes on my knees and ankles, everything feels revolted by hauling him up.

I'm regretting helping this asshole.

But I don't want him dead.

I want him *humiliated*.

I want the world to see him for what he is.

I want his face below headlines that read WORST PERSON EVER.

I want his name scorned in the boardrooms. Investors fleeing his companies. A financial bankruptcy to match his moral one.

I want the Salvation Army shelters to hang up pictures of his face by the door, captioned NOPE.

I want him to lose everything. *Everything*.

I want hard-core KKK Klansmen to spit on his starving, wretched husk as he weeps for all he's lost.

And I want to laugh.

With the aid of the rope, Noah heaves his chest and gut up onto a just barely submerged slab of rock. He pants gluttonously, not letting himself empty his lungs before trying to cram more air in. The asshole breathes like he does everything else.

"Beaks," Bradley says in my earpiece, "what the *fuck* are you playing at?"

"Do you have Deke?" I say.

"Unbuckling him now. But what the *literal* fuck are you doing?"

Noah's crawling up to his knees now, hoisting his flabby frame upright, still trying to catch his breath.

I sit back on my shelf. Noah's face is level with my shoulder, close enough to touch, if I could bring myself to do it. He's absolutely soaked and bedraggled, his oversized Hawaiian shirt glued to his corpulent gut.

I stare at Noah as he catches his breath.

"Harness coming down now," Bradley says.

"Ack."

Noah finally manages to stop hyperventilating, falling back to panting. "Told you," he wheezes. "Some people… are more valuable… than others."

I don't even think.

My left hand comes up, wrist to my ear as if I'm listening to an old-fashioned wristwatch, elbow cocked up behind my head. My fractured ribs howl their outrage. Half a second later, my hand flashes down as I exhale, fingers tucked tight against each other, pinky a line of muscled tension.

It's textbook technique: knife hand, reverse delivery.

Straight to Noah's Adam's apple.

Cartilage crunches beneath.

Noah rocks on his knees. His eyes are wide and bloodshot, his mouth an O of surprise and mortal fear. He clutches at his ruined throat, trying to bring air in through his shattered windpipe.

He never will.

My strike and asphyxiation steal his balance. Noah rolls to the side. Plunges into the water.

The orange life preserver stays visible, bouncing off one rock, then crashing into another.

Hitting the edge of the waterfall.

And vanishing.

I'm breathing heavy myself. My heart won't slow. On top of all my other injuries, the strike wrenched something in the pinky side of my hand.

I'm not going to see Noah suffer.

I think I'll survive the disappointment.

And it turns out that I *am* okay with killing a helpless person. Sometimes.

"Okay, you can play at that," Bradley says as I reach for the dangling harness. "But we gotta talk. That knife hand, B-plus technique. At best."

72

Thirty-four days later.

This private island a few miles off Malaysia is a rich man's playground. The beaches are fine sand that gently polishes the calluses from your feet as you walk. It's guarded seasonally by clouds of really nasty jellyfish, with schools of temperamental barracuda in the off season. The days are sunny and warm, with enough salt breeze to keep us comfortable even when the heat could crush anyone.

The main building perches atop a well-worn extinct volcano, a hard nub of rock a couple hundred feet above the water. There's a whole mess of elevators ranging from Industrial Behemoth to Victorian Luxury, plus a glass-walled cable car that goes straight down to the swimming beach. The last tsunami that came through here didn't even make it halfway up. The house is light and airy wood, gleaming hardwood and slate floors and huge ballrooms and bedrooms big enough to be called ballrooms.

A staff that's happy to serve. What's more, I can relax—they're not only well-compensated, they expect respect. They're all refugees from one conflict or another, offered safety and shelter. Offend the staff, and the island's owner will send you swimming with the jellyfish.

You'd expect the owner to be a villain from a Bond movie.

Once upon a time, it was.

Jacka tells me that the previous owner disappeared under mysterious circumstances. While a suspicious auditor might find some minor inconsistencies in how the current owner came to acquire title to the place, it's no worse than any other transfer of property in this part of the world. And nobody sees the real owner, anyway. Jacka's very specific that he doesn't own the place.

Which is totally bogus. He owns it. Well, most of it.

I could slap Jacka for having so much when others have so little. But what Jacka doesn't own the staff does, and they get the rest when he dies.

There are worse systems.

And it's best the staff doesn't know that Jacka's the real owner. They guess, I'm sure. His references to "the owner" don't fool anyone. But they're not *sure*.

And I have to admit that the Evil Villain Command Center under the basement is pretty sweet. The only people who could afford to buy this place would put it to far worse use.

Most important for us, there's a small but well-equipped medical center. The on-site nurse practitioner looks after the minor stuff. Deke and I arrived to find a whole medical staff from the mainland waiting for us, surrounding a trauma specialist and a general surgeon. Seems Jacka runs his own Witness Protection Program.

If he'd stop flirting outrageously with attached women, I'd be stuck liking him.

As it is, I'm only grateful.

I'm on this sweeping balcony, shaded by a broad bamboo awning. I'm back in the splits, my calves and thighs comfortable against the warm but not hot stone floor. The breeze off the Indian Ocean smells of salt and fish and countless trees and plants and all the parts of life. My ribs still ache, and my back still twinges when I bend too far backwards. But I'm comfortable enough stretched out here, a new large-screen tablet for my latest comics. (I'm trying to get into the Hellblazer reboot, but they've really messed up Constantine. I mean, *no*.) My white terrycloth shorts are long enough for decency, barely, and my pale blue shirt exposes my bellybutton.

I wouldn't normally dress like that.

But Deke enjoys the hell out of it.

Right now he's in a chaise, feet stretched out in front of him. His cheek looks better. He'll need plastic surgery later, but the infection's cleared out and the scar is the bright red and brown of healing tissue. His hair is thickening again. His mouth hangs a little bit open, exposing a whole row of temporary caps. His right hand holds a five-pound weight that he keeps lifting and lowering, flexing his bicep, rebuilding his strength.

And he can't take his eyes off me.

My bear deserves a thrill after all he's been through.

The doctor says no exercise, at all. No, not even that. He might rupture something.

But from the look in Deke's eye, that restriction isn't going to hold much longer.

My face is a little pink, and not just from the warm morning sun.

I need to find a tighter shirt. Maybe Tricia, the skin-and-bones assistant chef, can help me out.

The double glass doors leading into the mansion swing open. "This way," Jacka says, holding the door with his back and one hand stretched out towards us. You'd never know he'd been shot a month before—yes, he's gaunt, and pale, and looks like he doesn't eat nearly enough, but he always looks like that.

Well, always for the last few years, at least. Since he got shot in the gut, and Deke saved his life, and he started flirting only with married women.

But Rob comes right behind him. The dark skin of his face has picked up a few extra lines, and his close-cropped tightly curled hair a little more white, but beneath that he practically glows with well-rested health.

Bradley's on his heels. She's got a bruise on her cheekbone, but a narrow smile that she's just barely chained back. She can't give a big smile—it would hurt her reputation as Dame Brick of the famed You're Already Dead Estates.

"Rob!" Deke pulls himself to his feet. He's a lot stronger now, thanks to long walks and a dedicated physical therapist and a steady diet of as much high protein food as he can cram into his gut.

I add my greetings to the hubbub.

Jacka's gaze catches on me stretching. He tries to look on past, but gives this little nervous twitch. He needs a distinct effort of will to pull his attention up, and his voice is a little too fast when he says, "Come on, Betty, right on in."

The little Filipino kitchen lady isn't really named Betty, but it's the closest our clumsy American tongues can pronounce it. I got her to say her name probably a dozen times over our first week, but my efforts left her shaking her head and smiling.

I pull myself out of the stretch, letting the blood pour back into my warmed muscles. By the time I can stand, Betty has a gleaming chrome serving cart up next to the mosaic-topped table. Jacka's arranged cold fresh fruit juices: orange, papaya, mango, all from trees on the island. Slices of chilled fruit, vats of tea, crackers, tiny sandwiches like we're living in the British Raj.

"Thank you, Betty," Jacka says.

"You are most welcome," Betty says. She speaks English with just a hint of an accent. "Miss Salton, you have about two minutes."

"Thanks, Betty." I glance at Deke, then at Rob and Bradley. "Excuse me just a minute."

"We come across the world to greet you," Rob says, "and you immediately dash off?" His eyebrows narrow. "That's most unlike you."

"Can't avoid it," I say. "I don't want this place to catch on fire. If I'd known you were coming, I would have scheduled better." Ignoring Rob's puzzlement and Bradley's eye-rolling, I hide my smile until I'm out of sight.

By the time I come back, pushing the door open with my back, they're all settled in canvas director's chairs around the round wire-frame table, elbows on the intricate red and brown mosaic, drinks in hand. Bradley and Jacka are flanking Deke, who's laughing.

It's so good to see Deke laugh.

We have a long way to go. He still cries out in his sleep.

But when reach I out to take his hand and tell him it'll be all right, he settles down into our sheets.

We'll make it.

Jacka sees me backing the door open and leaps to his feet. "Pardon me, ma'am. Do please take my seat."

Jacka's at it again. I bet he deliberately took the chair next to Deke just so he could give it up. I let it pass—it's not time to strike back. Not yet. Instead, I hold my mittened hands high, displaying my treasure. "Be careful, hot tray coming through."

Rob now looks seriously confused. "My dear Beaks, what have you been doing?"

I set the nine-by-thirteen transparent blue baking pan on the stone tabletop. "Don't touch it, it's right from the oven."

Bradley leans in. "Brownies?"

"With pecans," I say. "I believe the exact phrase was, 'brownies or nothing, bitch.'"

Bradley blinks before exploding into laughter.

Rob says, "Mister Jacka. Dominic. I asked you to keep our arrival a surprise."

"I did not say you were coming," Jacka says.

Rob cocks an eyebrow.

Jacka shrugs, raising open hands. "I did *happen* to mention to Miss Salton that today would be a nice day to bake brownies. For one o'clock."

Rob shakes his head. "Apparently your confidence is only obtainable in matters of life and death. I will remember that."

"And money," Jacka says. "Don't forget money." He holds a glass towards me. "Cold drink?"

I accept a glass of chilled mango juice. I don't usually touch fruit juice—it's all sugar—but I've been working out a lot lately, and besides, it's a party. "What brings you out here?" I ask.

"Brownies," Bradley says.

"While they cool, then," I say.

"After all that trouble," Rob says, "we wanted to check on you and Deke."

"I'm better," Deke says. His hand finds my bare thigh beneath the table and gives a gentle squeeze. He doesn't have all his strength back, but his grip still thrills me.

No, the doctor says no exercise, dammit. If that rule's getting broken, let Deke start it. He needs to heal.

"We visited the hospital yesterday," I say. "Another round of MRIs—seems the people who own this joint bought a MRI machine for them."

Bradley eyes Jacka suspiciously. "Generous of him."

Jacka shrugs. "Whoever it is. Might be a woman. But yeah."

"It came out fine," Deke says. "Lots of PT ahead." His voice becomes dry. "Amazing how much cardio you lose, lying on your back for two weeks."

I put my hand over his, anchoring his hand on my leg. "You'll enjoy it."

"Enjoy it?" He eyes me. "You're going to be able to throw me around the mats for a couple months still."

"Like I said," I say. "You'll enjoy it."

Another chorus of laughter.

"By the way, Jacka," I say.

Petite cucumber sandwich half in his mouth, Jacka pauses and looks at me.

"The hospital director, Miss Wilke, met us as we were leaving the hospital."

"Nice lady," Jacka says. "Hope you gave her my best." He chomps down on the sandwich and chews.

"She was saying how much she appreciates all you've done for the hospital," I continue.

"Not me," he says around his full mouth. "Owner of this place."

"Still," Deke says. Merry hell burns in his eyes.

"We got to talking. Life's hard for a lady here in a position of authority." I keep my tone light. "Most of the men she meets don't respect a woman who's fought her way up, and most of those in her own social class are, frankly, assholes."

Jacka's almost done chewing, about to swallow. I have to finish this up.

"I know you admire her, so… you've got a dinner date for tomorrow."

Jacka jackknifes, doing a perfect spit-take straight into his lap. I get a quick thrill of victory before he wheezes, "You—" cough "—*what*?"

Bradley looks puzzled. Rob can't hide a sudden faint smirk.

"Set you up," Deke says. "With a woman."

"A real, live woman," I say.

"Talented," Deke says.

"Highly educated," I say.

"Worth knowin'," Deke says.

"Accomplished," I say.

Jacka sputters "But you can't—I can't—"

Comprehension illuminates Bradley's face. "You mean you'll talk a good game, but when it comes right down to it, you wimp out?"

Jacka draws himself up. "Wimp out?"

Bradley leans in. "Wimp. Out." She picks up a knife and tests the brownies. "You think these are cool enough to cut?"

"Should be," I say. "Jacka, you don't have to go."

"But if'n you don't show," Deke drawls, "she'll be disappointed. And you go out there a lot. Making donations and such."

"I'll help you pick out your clothes," I say. "Bring flowers. And for heaven's sake, trim that ear hair."

Jacka involuntarily raises a hand to an ear.

Rob says, "Pardon me, Beaks. Dominic, *I* will help you pick out your clothing. I do hope you own a decent suit."

"What's wrong with my taste?" I say.

"My dear Beaks," Rob says. "You dress like you're from Detroit."

"I am from Detroit."

"Exactly. Dominic does not need to be 'big pimping it,' as I believe the phrase goes." Rob's eyes turn appraisingly to Jacka. "He must look… distinguished."

"Fine," I say, throwing up my hands. "He's all in your hands. I'll text you the address. But being from Detroit, I'm saying: drive the Lotus."

Rob says, "Agreed."

Jacka looks horrified—but in amidst the fear, in his eyes there's just a faint little tingle of hope.

Everybody deserves hope. And the hope for love is the most important of them all.

"What about you, Rob?" Deke says. "You've got another big score coming, I'm sure?"

Rob leans back in the chair. "I fear not, my sweet Deke. I've talked things over with my husband." He glances around the table, gaze fixing on my face for just a second before continuing. "This last excursion persuaded me that my time in center stage has passed."

"You're retiring?" Deke says.

I want to argue, but I remember Rob's sallow face in those desperate moments. And in the jungle-choked Myanmar mountains, up against the Chinese border and down the river, we had too many desperate moments.

Freelancing is a young person's game.

"More… changing roles," Rob says. He knots his fingers across his chest. "I think it's time I try directing. That's another reason why I came out here."

Bradley raises a brownie. "Very nice." She runs her tongue across her teeth. "I think I came out ahead."

I give her a distracted nod. "What do you have in mind, Rob?"

"I'm evaluating a few scripts. Deke, once you're back in form again, I'll always have a role for you."

Deke smiles and ducks his head. I know he's worried about his career, after worrying about his legs and his head and all his other parts.

"The current production," Rob says, "has some openings. I'll need a brave driver who can also crew a Tivex-100 submarine."

"I'm in," Jacka says.

"Are you?" Rob raises an eyebrow. "I was of the impression you're afraid to take a charming woman out for an evening, and I clearly specified *brave*."

"Fine," Jacka snarls. "I'm in, after my—my date." He doesn't seem entirely displeased.

"Excellent." Rob turns to me. "We'll also need someone who can penetrate a building through its water system, cut their way out, climb an access shaft, and precisely bewilder alarm systems. The performance involves a firm that's skirted the law many times, and inflicted considerable harm on many communities around the world."

I glance at Deke. He gives a barely perceptible nod of his chin—not permission, but agreement. "We have some things to do first," Deke says, squeezing my thigh.

I turn back to Rob. "I think I know just the lady."

"Oh?" Bradley says around a mouth full of brownie. "Does she know explosives?"

"That's me," I say. "Making the world better, one explosion at a time."

Beaks Returns in *Terrapin Sky Tango*

Read on for a preview…

1

I need to scrub the blood off my reputation.

Yes, "mess with Beaks and she will utterly destroy everything you love" is a useful addition to it. And a rep should grow with you, developing fine notes and subtleties, so that it becomes worthy of a connoisseur's attention and a higher billing rate.

But a reputation is your best advertising. I can't put up billboards to broadcast my services. What would they say? *Beaks: She Steals, so You Don't Have To?* Maybe *Six Feet of Skinny Sneakiness?* Or *Limber. Lethal. Lawless.*

No, the only way people learn about me is by word of mouth.

Or the bulletin board at the local Interpol office.

Plus, I'm told there's an FBI agent that has my picture in his office, my smiling Mediterranean face over my real name: Billie Carrie Salton. And that he uses it as a dart board. But the person who told me that is kind of a suck-up, so who knows?

If it's true, it's adorable.

I've worked hard on the core of my rep: "They'll never know Beaks was there, until they realize something's missing." If you're a bloated rich bastard, you can hire me to rob some other bloated rich bastard. None of my clients think they're bloated rich bastards, of course, but here's a hint:

If you can afford me, you're bloated rich.

If you're thinking of hiring me, you're a bastard.

The one who hired me for this gig? Even more of a bastard. And not because of the thievery.

First: Arizona. No, not the nice cool mountains, but—ugh—Phoenix. North of Scottsdale, more precisely.

In August.

Even early in the day, before the sun's poked its head up above the mountains lining the valley, it seems the locals replaced the sky with an open-air incinerator. It's seven AM and I need another gallon of sunscreen. The light's bright enough to threaten my scalp beneath my inch-long hair. Four nights in this hellhole and I'm so dry my eyeballs hurt and the inside of my nose has cracked like I'm in close solar orbit. I can smell the dried-up traces of my own nosebleeds. I've already drunk a gallon of water just trying to keep the headache to a distant thud.

The few bushes and scrub trees scattered across the flat, dead ground have gone into some kind of weird summer hibernation. Even the cacti look shriveled. A couple of them have a sturdy wooden cage supporting them. I hear these particular cacti are a protected species, because the world doesn't have enough thorns.

We're standing at the east side of this useless intersection. A bunch of developers convinced the city council that the boom would never end and got them to approve this network of main roads in the desert. Four lane roads, of course, because everything grows forever and you want your city infrastructure to support all that growth, right? One square mile sections, so you can allocate chunks one after the other. And you'll want underground utilities, because they're storm-resistant and they cost more to install. Think of the tax base you'll get from all these homes and businesses! Oh, wait, there's an economic crash? Economies don't grow forever? Sorry, we'll take our fees for pouring all this concrete and shut up now.

The only thing traveling this road is blown sand.

The only sound: the faint grumble of traffic, thousands of gas-guzzlers and the shouts of frustrated drivers blended by distance.

Our rental car lurks behind us. It's a great big Old Rich People sedan, silver. The trunk is shut, but both front doors are open so we can leap in if we need to. I had to knock out the rear window when the bullet holes made the safety glass opaque.

We won't even have air conditioning until we get the hell out of this Hell.

A mile west I can make out the white line of the brick wall separating the cozy upper-middle-class condos from the wilderness. The limey reek of hot concrete already fills the air and it's not even proper daytime.

But if you want to exchange stolen goods for a suitcase of cash, and you don't want anyone sneaking up on you, this desolate intersection is perfect. The only man-made things in miles are the roads and a gray utility box sitting on the opposite corner like an abandoned bedroom dresser.

Next to me, Lou shifts uneasily.

Lou is the second problem. He's got to be twenty years older than me, at least mid-forties and probably pushing fifty, but in this business he's a newborn. Give him coveralls and a pipe wrench and he'd look like a Nintendo plumber. Maybe an older version, with the bits of gray salting his mustache.

I have no idea why Lou wants to be in the business. He'd tried to tell me, that first night, but I'd put him straight. Me knowing wouldn't help me and might hurt him. We freelance because we literally can't fit in anywhere else.

If you have a happy childhood, you don't do this kind of work.

Every one of us is a unique freak.

But we're in good company.

"Relax," I say. Lou is so nervous he looks like he's about to have his first prostate exam and fears he might enjoy it. "You did well so far."

"Well?" A voice that deep shouldn't crack quite that badly. "How many people shot at us last night?"

"Part of the job, sometimes." I study his outfit one last time. Three days ago he'd arrived in denim shorts, T-shirt, and baseball cap, but on our first day he'd swapped the cap for a floppy flow-through hat with a brim just short of sombrero. We'd spent most of the days afterwards posing as hikers to research our target. For the trade, I'd had him add sturdy slacks and a polo shirt, plus some sunglasses tougher than they looked. No, not darker—tougher.

Today called for unbreakable sunglasses. "The men after us last night, they worked for the man we robbed."

"We think." I've seen federal prosecutors look more trusting than Lou right now.

"Don't trust anything anyone says at gunpoint," I say. "Here, we're meeting our customer. Rules are, you don't bring a gun to the swap."

Lou glances up the south road. "Even if it wasn't the customer that was after us last night—are they going to follow that?"

"They'll have guns in their car." My lips tingle as I speak—they're a chapped ruin. Once we escape this level of Hell, I'm bathing in moisturizer for a week. "But they won't want to damage the goods. That's the whole point of this little game."

The breeze picks up, flowing through my outfit. My pants and shirt are a tough synthetic, breathable but difficult to cut through. It'll stop a knife slash. Won't do any good against a bullet, of course, but hopefully the shooting's done.

Until I say so, at least.

Plus, my pants have *pockets*. Screw you, fashion tycoons.

My earpiece buzzes. "Incoming," Deke says from his hidden nest. "White van, from the north."

"Thanks," I say. I've left my throat mic on—Lou and I won't be saying anything Deke can't hear. My Deke can hear anything I ever say. Last time I doubted Deke, he was tortured within an inch of his life.

That's when the blood got all over my reputation.

"Are we really going to return the car?" Lou says.

"When we're done."

"Won't the bullet holes make them—"

"That's what I bought all that rental insurance for." I raise a hand to shield the side of my face as I look north. I can't see anything yet, but a white van against the distant line of houses would disappear at half a mile. "Seriously, this isn't the time. It won't be an issue, I promise. We have to stay chill. Focus completely on the moment."

My phone buzzes with a text message.

Not my regular phone—the special one I wear on gigs. Maybe a dozen people in the world have that number.

I glance at the display on my wrist.

My brother Will.

Annoyance tightens my gut. Then I read the text.

FATHER IS DEAD.

2

I freeze like a tiny bug pinned to an endless beige display board.

The back of my neck flashes with heat as the first edge of the sun cracks the rounded mountains.

The text message's three words crank my headache up to eleven to thud in my temples. My parched eyes should tear up from the thunderous pounding. No, I probably have tears, but the ridiculous dry heat is sucking it away before they can run. My mouth is somehow even more arid, though.

How could Dad be dead?

I hadn't seen him since I started college, fourteen years ago. He'd tried to see me when I graduated with the triple bachelor's, but it hadn't gone well. And Father had been well on his way down Cirrhosis Highway back then, racing pedal-down towards Lung Cancer Junction.

I'd always imagined Cirrhosis Highway looked a lot like this barren desert, with straggly shrubs barely hanging on and a few grains of loose sand skittering across the hardpack. Father's road had Jack Daniels bottles instead of useless storm drains, though, and ditches full of Marlboro stubs.

Okay, I know perfectly well how he can be dead. Dumb question.

If he was that sick, though, why hadn't William let me know earlier? The idiot was supposed to be watching over Father.

"What's wrong?" Lou says.

I feel dizzy.

Breathe. I need to breathe.

Father's death had to be an accident.

Or slow alcohol-and-tobacco suicide.

I push the air out of my frozen lungs and deliberately pull in a deep breath. "Nothing." Another breath. The flat smell of drought-scorched earth fills my nose. "Nothing."

"Billie?" Deke says in my ear.

"Later," I hiss.

For Father, there is no later. There's only never.

A voice in the back of my head screams that I should have taken a chance to 'set things right' between us. But there wasn't anything to set right. Father is, *was* a drunk. He'd chased Mom off the Christmas I was ten, and she hadn't taken anything but her remaining teeth. Without Uncle Carl and Aunt Pat, his drinking would have taken me down with him.

I could have changed nothing.

I should have changed everything.

"Beaks!" Lou hisses.

I jerk.

A cargo van slows as it approaches the intersection, its pristine windowless white flanks glaring with early sunlight. The words TERRAPIN TRANSPORT gleam in bright blue on the flank, atop a grinning green turtle. A tinted windshield conceals the driver, but that's not suspicious. Scottsdale's in the running for Tinted Glass Capital of the United States.

I will myself to breathe. Inflating my paralyzed lungs takes concentration.

A couple yards short of the stop sign, the van pulls to the side, blocking my view of the drab gray utility box sticking out of the opposite lot.

The exchange is on.

Focus, woman! I fumble at my pants. The radio beacon makes a thin rectangular shape in my pocket. I push the "on" button through the smooth cloth and hear a low-pitched beep.

We're ready.

I deliberately relax my shoulders and unclench my hands. Father isn't a problem anymore. Hell, now that I'm not supporting him, I can keep all the money from this gig.

The thought doesn't help the voiceless burn in my heart.

Besides, there'll be funeral expenses. It's not like my brother has that kind of money. Or any money.

The van driver opens his door and hops out.

He's a stubby man, with baby-smooth skin above a harsh black five o'clock shadow, broad muscular shoulders, and a ghastly pale complexion that almost mirrors the sizzling sunlight. Dressed for the office, complete with a ridiculous short-sleeved white button-up shirt and fire-engine-red tie, he steps towards me with an incredibly well-balanced stride. It's like he expects an earthquake, but doesn't want it to knock the invisible ledger off of his head. His hands are open, relaxed, and empty. A bright red baseball cap with a white eagle-head logo on the front casts a vital line of shade over his naked eyes.

Basically, he's the exact opposite of Father.

Focus, focus, focus. "Stabinowitz." I raise my voice to carry the words across the intersection. "I thought I'd see you."

His toothy white grin reflects the sunrise almost as well as a mirror. "We've been around too long to stand on formalities, Miss Beaks. Please call me Joe. And what was your first hint?" He sounds like he's been awake for hours, and waiting all of them for a chance to strike up a conversation with a pretty blonde.

Fortunately, I'm a brunette today. "Joe it is, then. And it's just Beaks. Last night we came across a gentleman who'd had a butter knife inserted into his brain through his eye socket, and I asked myself 'who could do that?'"

Joe raised his shoulders and spread his hands. "Guilty. To be fair, he was trying to shoot me."

"I assumed as much." Stabbity Joe's skill with knives is both legendary, and his weakness. He's faster than me, and he practices with knives the way Father practiced with Pabst—*no, no, no. You just yelled at Lou to stay in the moment. Take your own advice.*

Stabbity Joe's hands are empty. He's wearing short sleeves, so the most obvious knife cache is gone. They've got to be in his pockets, or maybe down the back of his collar—no, that collar looks tight underneath his tie.

A gust of wind skitters sand past us. Joe's tie doesn't flutter.

That's one knife, then. He'll have a bunch more, hidden somewhere nastily clever.

Not as nasty as when Father got mad at the neighbor and—*no, stop it stop it stop it.*

"Who's your friend?" Stabbity Joe says.

I don't look at Lou, but he doesn't answer. Just like I told him.

"My problem," I say.

"Nice to meet you, My Problem." Stabbity Joe grins like that's funny.

"If you want to banter, Joe, then let's get this deal done and go to a bar," I say. "Ten minutes from now, this place is going to be even more of a hellhole."

His grin grows. "Don't tell me our desert is too much for you?"

Our? He's from a desert—maybe this desert. Or is he playing at leaking information? "You and I both know Phoenix was founded because this is where the settlers' last camel died. We stand here twenty minutes, we join it."

I need to seem impatient, but not too impatient.

This conversation needs to stretch until I get Deke's signal.

"Indeed." Joe slowly rotates on his axis to scan the horizon, pointedly spreading his arms farther as he turns his back to me. "I do believe we are quite alone, Beaks."

"Then bring it out." Those stupid verbal games would remind me of family any day, not just today, but my voice is still harder than it should be.

Cool, girl.

Collected.

Present. In the moment.

"Candy!" Stabbity Joe calls.

The van clanks.

I sense Lou's weight shift and suppress a wince. If Lou freaks out and starts anything, I'll have to put him down before Joe gets a chance to go all stabbity.

The side of Joe's van slides smoothly open, the sound of its motion barely audible above the breeze. I'm watching the dark interior, but also keeping an eye on the edges of the van and trying to peer into the shadowed space beneath it. Deke will warn us about another car coming in, but if Joe had seen Cape Fear one too many times and arrived with a shooter dangling from the undercarriage, this would be a good moment for him to strike.

Stabbity Joe was mostly honorable. In this business, freelancers who are willing to blow up the exchange pick up the kind of nasty stink that's real hard to get rid of. Don't get me wrong, he'd kill you if that was the job, but he'd do it properly. From behind, when you weren't expecting it.

But still, I had to be as watchful as when I'd been a kid and—

No.

That was petty shit. It's done. I'm the best in my business now, and Father's a lump of meat.

The hammering heat-headache threatens to knock my noggin off my neck. Better to think of that. Better still to watch the van. Just because Stabbity Joe was known to be basically okay didn't mean that he couldn't be offered enough to mow me down.

And Lou, yeah.

But mostly me.

Someone faintly says *oof.*

A scrawny woman with a tangle of dark hair flowing down past her shoulders clambers out of the van's dim interior. She turns her back to us, reaches inside, and heaves out a cardboard box plastered with the Amazon logo.

I hear good things about Amazon, but I'm never home to get packages.

Maybe Deke and I should steal a home one day.

"Prime Pantry," Stabbity Joe says. "The greatest boxes made today."

What? "The box is fine. What's in the box is the question."

Stabbity Joe steps aside, leaving room for Candy to pass.

She looks too scared to be a professional freelancer. Those denim shorts are too short, and the Arizona State T-shirt is way too tight. And any double-D needs to be wearing a bra—

Realization slaps me. "Joe, I thought we were professionals."

Joe gives that annoying pick-up smile. "She is a professional."

How *dare* he bring some random civilian into this? Is he really that stupid? "Not that sort of pro and you know it."

"It's an easy job," Joe says. "I'll eat my second-best Bowie if Mister My Problem there is any less green than my Miss Candy. And don't worry, she's being very well-compensated for her time."

Candy squints against the light at my back, and I feel like an asshole. Yes, I'd chosen to put the sun at my back as an advantage during the exchange, but a pro would have brought eye protection. She only has an arch of purple above each eye, making the sockets seem huge. At each sun-pained blink, glitter flashes on her darkened eyelids. Her lips are a tight line of fire engine red.

Candy's pretty clearly accustomed to working nights, when the artificial light and pancake makeup can hide the bruise on her left cheek. There's another on her left temple.

I'm not one of those moralizing assholes who thinks that women shouldn't do whatever they must to survive.

I'm one of those moralizing assholes who thinks you shouldn't beat people who are willing to sleep with you, even if they do it for money.

Mom covered up her bruises like that.

Fury blazes.

No, not now.

Survive the swap.

An hour from now, you can break down and scream and cry and whatever you need to do.

But right now, survive the swap.

Candy's slow pace doesn't come from her ghastly do-me glitter heels. She's terrified.

"You can't tell me she wants to be here," I say.

Stabbity Joe says, "You remember the gentleman with the butter knife?"

Candy flinches.

Stabbity Joe says, "He incapacitated my partner. I was forced to find a substitute, at short notice. That's far enough, Miss Candy."

Candy finishes her step and halts, square in the middle of the intersection. A racing car coming from any direction could mow her down.

Fortunately, the endless empty road stretching in all four directions would give her plenty of warning.

I wave Lou forward, into the intersection.

Candy hands Lou the box.

Lou sits on his heels so he can inspect the contents of the box. Counting should take between four and five minutes, but his impressively deft fingers finish leafing through the Panamanian bearer bonds in maybe three and a half. I hope it's because he's good, not because his attention slipped partway through. He folds the top of the box shut and stands to give me a nod.

"Good," I say. "The Duke's in the trunk."

3

Once the action starts, Lou's great at following directions. That's not enough to join this business, but it's sure a prerequisite. Lou retreats from the neutral intersection and heads to the bullet-scarred rental car behind me. I hear a click as he pops the trunk, then a huff as he heaves the Grand Duke out.

We'd had to drop the rear seats to get the Duke's case into the trunk.

Cellos are *not* small.

And better Lou looks towards the sun than me. My sinuses are so dry they ache, and sunscreen or no, I'm pretty sure this gig is going to scorch my olive skin to red. It's not only the sun—even the *sky* is brutal. Lou's mustache and his big hat would give him more protection than my sunglasses.

Besides, experience has its privileges. Let the new guy get the sunburn.

Stabbity Joe's still standing back by his van, about thirty feet away, with battered Candy at the halfway point. All nice and proper.

"You know, Joe," I say loudly, "since we've both been around a while, I think I should tell you that this gig hasn't gone well."

"Oh?" Stabbity Joe grins. "I'd love to hear about it some time."

"The thing is, this is the third time I've stolen this same cello. Each time it's been better guarded than the time before."

"It's a special one, I hear."

Lou comes up past me, humping the most ridiculously sturdy cello case I've ever seen. It's nearly as big as he is, the steel trim shining white over black bulletproof polymer. James Bond once rode an open cello case down a mountain, with a girl in his lap and the cello in hers. It's not an instrument you'd want to try to squeeze through an air duct.

Plus, the protective case is damn heavy.

"Stradivarius' Grand Duke," I say. "Commissioned in the summer of 1723 by the Grand Duke of Tuscany, but not completed until 1724 after the Duke was dead. One of his finest instruments."

Stabbity Joe purses his lips. "You sure read a lot."

I flashback to Father snatching *Surely you're Joking, Mister Feynman* out of my hands and screaming at me to get the goddamn dishes done. I was nine. My throat catches, and a little shudder traverses my spine.

I can't let any of that leak into my voice—we're already in enough danger.

"Here's the thing," I say. "That first time, I stole it from Colin Baywater. Last night, I stole it from him again."

Stabbity Joe laughs. "Really? That's fucking hilarious."

"I'm glad you think so. But the number of people who really care about cellos, and who have the wherewithal to hire me, is pretty small. I'm guessing there's only two."

Stabbity Joe laughs even louder. "I was wrong. *That's* fucking hilarious. You think our employer had you *re*-steal it."

"I'm a contractor. You're the employee." The last time someone offered me employment I blew up his home, his boat, and his private prison. "And I don't know that."

Lou's got the black cello case all the way into the intersection, about three feet from Candy. He kneels. Brass latches click, barely audible above the grumble of millions of frustrated commuters on the miles-distant freeway.

I say, "The point is, if you could do me a favor? Tell your boss that if I'm right, the next time he calls me, I'm going to have to tack on a stupidity tax."

Lou flips the case open.

"Don't tell me you wouldn't take the job?" Stabbity Joe says in mock surprise.

Lou reaches into the case and hoists the Grand Duke up for inspection, holding it by the slender curved neck.

The varnished wood gleams brown and red. The steel tuning keys are painfully bright in the sunlight. Lou hasn't put the end pin in, of course, so the base rests inside the heavy padded case. He spins the front towards Stabbity Joe, displaying the raised frets and the F holes.

"Check it," Stabbity Joe says.

Candy jumps.

The faded memory of my mom leaping before Father could throw a slap echoes up from the dusty bottom of my mind. My teeth clench.

"Quickly, now!" Stabbity Joe says. He's not angry, but my memories dance.

Candy takes a couple steps to cross in front of the Grand Duke. Her hands flutter as if she's going to touch it, but she yanks them back to her sides. She's been told not to touch the merchandise. She kneels and studies the front.

The Grand Duke has a little notch next to the fret, where Angelo Stucci's bow slipped during an especially frenetic performance in 1881. And the left-hand F-hole has a strangely curved edge of unknown provenance. Scholars' best guess is that some ham-fisted carpenter attempted "repairs" sometime between 1821 and 1823.

Candy stands. She offers Stabbity Joe two thumbs up.

"Beaks," Stabbity Joe says. "Could you ask My Problem there to turn the Duke around for us?"

I told Lou to expect the request. He obliges.

Candy crouches. The X grain should show up near the neck, and there's three parallel scrapes off to the right-hand side. Old Stucci was rough on his instruments.

This instrument is remarkable. I imagine it sounds glorious.

Not that I listen to classical music. Give me some Savages or Screaming Females and I'm good all day.

Candy hops back up and offers another two thumbs up. Even through the makeup, I can see her face has lost even more color. She's too afraid to shake.

Her terror is too familiar, and right now it's too raw. "Miss Candy," I say.

Stabbity Joe says, "Any instructions you want to give her, you tell me."

"It's not an instruction." I turn my attention back to Candy. "Anything you say, it can leak information. If Joe was going to kill you, he wouldn't have told you to be silent. Stay calm, follow instructions, and you'll make it home just fine."

Candy's face stills. Have I reassured her?

Or is she now so scared she's completely shut down?

"Pep talks for my people?" Stabbity Joe says. The light is so harsh, his five-o-clock shadow stands out like black paint on his pallid face.

"I want everyone here to get home alive and with a few extra dollars in their pocket," I say.

Joe's eyes stay hard, but his lips flirt with a teasing smile. "The rumors are right. You're a softy."

"Incoming," Deke whispers in my ear. "One west, one north, both at high speed."

His words give me a warm thrill of satisfaction. We're running out of time.

I'm at my best when I'm out of time.

My pulse picks up a notch, pushing my headache back. "I believe in punching up. Punching up hard. Satisfied?"

"Oh, yes."

To Lou I say, "Hand over the cello and grab my bearer bonds."

Right on schedule, the cello's neck shatters into a billion pieces.

The sound of the gunshot arrives a quarter-second later.

What happens next? Grab *Terrapin Sky Tango* to find out!

About the Author

https://mwl.io

Never miss another new release!

Sign up for Michael Warren Lucas' mailing list at

http://mwl.io.

Novels:

Immortal Clay

Kipuka Blues

Butterfly Stomp Waltz

Terrapin Sky Tango

Hydrogen Sleets

git commit murder

Nonfiction (as Michael W Lucas):

Relayd and Httpd Mastery – PAM Mastery – FreeBSD Mastery: Advanced ZFS – FreeBSD Mastery: Specialty Filesystems – FreeBSD Mastery: ZFS – Tarsnap Mastery – Networking for Systems Administrators – FreeBSD Mastery: Storage Essentials – Sudo Mastery – DNSSEC Mastery – Absolute OpenBSD – SSH Mastery – Network Flow Analysis – Absolute FreeBSD – Cisco Routers for the Desperate – PGP & GPG –FreeBSD Mastery: Jails –Ed Mastery

See your favorite bookstore for more!